KATHRYN LASKY

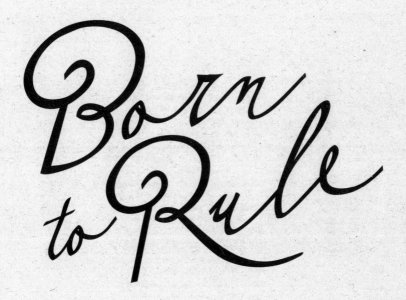

Born to Rule

A
CAMP PRINCESS
NOVEL

HARPERCOLLINS*PUBLISHERS*

Library of Congress Cataloging-in-Publication
Data is available.
ISBN-10: 0-06-058761-X (trade bdg.)
ISBN-13: 978-0-06-058761-1 (trade bdg.)
ISBN-10: 0-06-058763-6 (pbk. bdg.)
ISBN-13: 978-0-06-058763-5 (pbk. bdg.)

Typography by Sasha Illingworth
1 2 3 4 5 6 7 8 9 10
❖
First Edition

Born to Rule

CAMP PRINCESS SCHEDULE

8:15 Rise and be splendid

8:30 Breakfast in bed

10:00 Swimming (weather dependent), songbird catching, falconry, lawn tennis, or (in case of poor weather) needlepoint

11:00 Snacks in the Princess Parlor

11:45 Makeup in Salon de Beauté, canoeing, sailing, riding, or archery

1:00 Luncheon (midday tiaras required)

2:30 Jewel crafts (bring your favorite family gems)

3:30 Quiet time in the turrets

4:00 High tea (tea gowns and tea tiaras required)

5:00 Free time

6:15 Ladies' maids report to turrets for dressing of princesses for dinner

8:00 Dinner

9:30 Evening activities

10:15 Candles snuffed. Princess taps.

CAMP PRINCESS STAFF

CAMP MISTRESS:
Queen Mother Adelia Elsinore Louisa of Palacyndra

**MISTRESS OF THE AVIARY &
SONGBIRD COUNSELOR:**
Princess Roseanna

MAKEUP & COSMETICS COUNSELOR:
The Duchess of Bagglesnort

TAPESTRY COUNSELOR:
Lady Merry von Schleppenspiel

**MASTER OF THE HAWKS &
FALCONRY COUNSELOR:**
Gamphery of Lochlin

WATERFRONT COUNSELORS:
Lady Gustavia, Princess Lily Padinsky

MASTER OF THE STABLES:
Moncrieff of Sullamore

DANCE COUNSELOR:
Luigi Pippinia

LORE AND MORE COUNSELOR:
Lady Elaine

**RIDING COUNSELOR &
HEAD UNICORN WRANGLER:**
Lady Frances ("Frankie")

CAMP NURSE:
Nurse Bodkin

ARCHERY MASTER:
Hawkins of Sherwood

Each princess camper is required to bring the following:

GOWNS

- 6 morning gowns suitable for indoor activities
- 6 morning gowns suitable for outdoor activities, two of which should be all-white for tennis
- 6 tea gowns
- 12 evening-wear gowns suitable for banquets and evening light entertainments
- 12 ball gowns for major balls, dances, and more formal activities

SMALLCLOTHES

- 8 under-kirtles
- 5 over-kirtles
- 6 under-tunics
- 18 pairs of hose (6 cotton, 6 silk, 6 wool)
- 9 chemises or smocks

- 3 dozen shifts
- 18 petticoats
- 24 pantalettes
- night rails for sleeping—simple cambric preferred rather than silk

SPORTS COSTUMES

- 20 overtunics for outdoor sports. These may be worn over kirtles or sports pantaloons.
- Bathing costumes and tiaras shall be provided.
- Riding skirts
- Riding boots
- Falconry gloves shall be provided.

HEADGEAR

- 6 short veils—we ask that veils of the modern design be sent. They should be no longer than 12 inches and flow off the back of the head and not cover the face. This is crucial for safety during outdoor sports.
- Broad-brimmed hats made from rushes to protect from the sun (available at a steep discount in the *Royal Campers' Equipment Catalogue*)
- 1 coronet bearing the heraldic seal of the princess's country

- 2 lightweight sports tiaras (no heraldry required)
- 3 jeweled hairnets for dress

SHOES
- Ballet slippers
- Ballroom dancing slippers (no buckles please, only ribbons for fastening)
- High suede, leather, or calfskin fleece-lined boots for outdoor activites in winter

OUTERWEAR
- 2 cloaks
- 3 mantles or pelisses
- 4 shawls
- oiled sheepskin cape for rainwear
- 10 pairs of gloves (4 lace, 2 pigskin, 3 silk, 1 heavy leather)

PERSONAL EQUIPMENT
- Toilet articles (perfume, bath salts, toothbrushes)
- Bed linens
- Blankets
- Towels
- Prayer book
- Heraldic stamp and wax for sealing letters

OPTIONAL PERSONAL EQUIPMENT

- Paint sets
- Dolls, teddy dragons, family pictures, etc.
- Jewelry
- Writing materials
- Books
- Bows and arrows (although we do provide them for archery, some campers prefer their own)

Please make sure that your camping princess has received a copy of the *Camp Princess Handbook* and has read it thoroughly before her arrival.

Parents are encouraged to send a modest amount of gold that shall be deposited in the Camp Princess coffers and can be used for small purchses at the camp store—candy, perfumes, fletching materials for those who prefer to fletch their own arrows, sealing wax, etc.

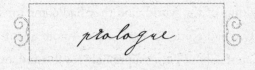

A ROYAL PROCESSION

It was Gilly, the lady's maid, who saw them first. "Here they come!" she called, and nudged Mary, the chambermaid, who stood next to her on the watchtower. Gilly squinted at the bright ribbon of color winding down the high road. Forty of the most royal princesses on earth were coming to Camp Princess, riding on horses and in carriages. Their splendid banners snapped in the wind and their jeweled tiaras flashed in the sun as they rode toward the castle. Servants—from the chambermaids and the footmen to the mistresses of the wardrobe and the gamekeepers—tried to get a glimpse. Gilly sighed happily. The procession seemed to grow richer and more beautiful every year.

Here were the daughters from some of the most splendid kingdoms of the world, and they had come for summer camp. They had come to learn more—more about being a princess, more about being supremely royal—and, of course, to have fun of the most royal variety.

A tremor of excitement passed through the servants as they heard the creak and clank of the drawbridge being lowered. Even the fish jumped from the sparkling waters of the moat as if trying to catch a peek at the new royal campers. Gilly stuck her hand in her apron and touched her lucky stone.

Please! Please! Please, lucky stone, bring nice princesses, lovely princesses, kind princesses to the South Turret. Not snotty ones like last summer.

NEW ARRIVALS

Princess Alicia of All the Belgravias dismounted her pony and stepped into the courtyard. It was her first season at Camp Princess, and her heart was beating as frantically as a hummingbird's. She was used to being surrounded by her sisters, cousins, and servants. But now, as she stood in this throng of laughing, happy princesses she didn't know, she felt very much alone. Alicia was glad when a tall woman with a crown took charge.

"Princesses, Princesses, may I have your attention? Please be quiet while I announce your turret assignments in the royal castle of Camp Princess. When your title is called, kindly step up to the footman and receive your welcome scroll."

"That is the Queen Mum," another princess said to Alicia. "She is Camp Mistress." Alicia smiled at the girl and moved in closer to listen for her name. If they went in alphabetical order, she would certainly be one of the first to be called. But alas, the assignments were by turret.

"East Turret, Princess Zelenka from the Dominion of Thrallnork, Princess Parisiana from the Majestic Realm of Chantillip . . ." The list went on. There were three girls assigned to each turret. After the East Turret came the North Turret and then the West Turret.

Princesses all around Alicia were chattering away. "I hope I'm not in the South Turret!" one princess exclaimed.

"Me too. I wouldn't want to live in a turret that has a ghost," another said.

"Is it true that your turretmates are also your team-mates?" someone else asked.

"I think so. Do you want to be a Purple or a Crimson? My sister was on the Crimson team, and they've won the Color Wars three years in a row. I really want to be a Crimson. There are all sorts of contests and competitions, you know, jewelry making, archery."

"I heard the Crimsons were all snotty," someone said.

"What's the first contest?" Alicia asked.

"I'm not sure, but the big one this session is the songbird competition. It counts for a lot. We only have two weeks to catch and train a songbird."

"Holy monk bones!" Alicia exclaimed. "That's not much time!"

"Look at her," Alicia heard one of the princesses whisper rather loudly and then point at a new arrival. "That feather in her riding cap—that is so over."

"So five minutes ago!" another said.

Alicia's stomach turned. She had a feather in one of her riding caps. Luckily she had not worn it today.

Just then she heard her name called. "South Turret, Princess Alicia of All the Belgravias, Princess Gundersnap of the Empire of Slobodkonia, Princess Kristen of the Isles of the Salt Tears in the Realm of Rolm."

A pretty princess with jet-black hair turned to another girl. "I'm glad I'm not them! I'd be afraid of the South Turret ghost!"

"Oh, heavens, Princess Rosamunde, that ghost is just a rumor from two hundred years ago!" the other princess answered confidently, though Alicia thought she saw her give a little shiver and look around quickly.

Ooh, I hope she's right, Alicia thought. She stepped

forward to receive her welcome scroll. It was a sheet of parchment rolled up and tied with a purple ribbon.

"This must mean we're on the Purple team—duh!" said the princess named Kristen, laughing. Tall and lanky, she was wearing very high, soft suede boots trimmed with fur. Her tiara was made from gold-dipped sawed-off antlers, and her fiery red hair was clipped with a barrette made of some sort of animal's tooth studded with sapphires. She wore not a wisp of silk or satin, but Alicia admitted that this princess was stylish in a barbaric sort of way.

Princess Gundersnap, on the other hand, seemed to be a complete disaster. She was stumpy and squat, with pimples and mud-colored hair that sprang out like corkscrews from under her iron tiara. Not a pretty sight! Alicia thought. She looked grumpy as well. Great, thought Alicia. Grumpy and stumpy—and then, of course, a stylish savage. Where do I fit in? She looked down at her own beautiful pink brocade riding skirt festooned with ribbons and lace, and wondered if she looked as odd to her turretmates as they did to her.

Just as Alicia was contemplating her predicament, she heard the Camp Mistress say, "Now, Princesses, in case you are of a mathematical inclination . . ."

"Math, no fair," said Princess Kristen in her lilting accent. "No schoolwork, just fun here."

"I agree!" said another. "I'm here for jewelry design and dances with Camp Burning Shield."

Burning Shield! Alicia had heard from her older sister, Lorelei, about the boys' camp across the lake. There were bunches of cute princes!

The Camp Mistress continued, "You will notice that there are forty princesses, and not all the turrets are the same size. We've done some juggling and doubling up, but it seems that with all my computations, we still have one turret with room for an additional one-third princess. All the others are full. So, you might ask, who is one-third a princess? Well, Your Highnesses, she is a full and royal princess, but she is quite small."

At that moment all eyes turned toward a truly tiny princess who wore a teeny-weeny tiara. She appeared rather frightened, and her eyes glistened with tears. She was the only one who had not been assigned a turret. "Princess Myrella of the Marsh Kingdoms, will you step forward, please?"

The tiny princess walked up to the Queen Mum, who bent way down and said, "My dear little princess of the Marsh Kingdoms, we shall squeeze you into North Turret." She handed her a rolled parchment with a purple ribbon.

"Fat lot of good she'll do the Purples," someone said in

a nasty voice. At that moment the eyes of the three princesses of the South Turret met.

"*Sctonken* meanie!" muttered Gundersnap.

"Go suck a conch!" Princess Kristen blurted.

"That is really royally rude of her to say!" exclaimed Princess Alicia.

The three young princesses looked at one another and knew in that moment that although they were different in many ways, they were the same in an important one. Their hearts went out to the teeny tiny Princess Myrella of the Marsh Kingdoms.

Chapter 2

HOMESICK

Alicia looked around her room. She'd brought small touches of home that reminded her of Belgravia. Her glass bottles with her best perfumes sat on the dressing table, and a painting of her royal family hung above her bed. Still, she missed her own castle, especially now that it was quiet time and she had a moment to think about things.

Some princesses brought their favorite stuffed animals to camp, but Alicia had her favorite book, *Love Letters of a Forgotten Princess*. It was a birthday present from her beloved aunt, the Queen of Albermarle. Almost every night she read at least one of the letters. It was on her nightstand now, adding a cozy touch to the room. Knowing it was there made Alicia feel just a bit less homesick.

She sat down at the gold writing table, chose a quill, and dipped it into the crystal inkwell.

> *Dear Mum and Pop (or HM and HRH),*
> *I think it is really stupid that they have this rule that I cannot call you Mum and Pop in a letter but must address you as Her Majesty and His Royal Highness. Why do they care what I call you in a letter? So I'm doing it both ways, which means that I'm not quite following and not quite breaking the rule.*
>
> *Well, I don't mean to complain but . . . guess what else? It's not summer. You told me that the weather was "odd" here, but holy monk bones, it's just started to snow! It was spring when we rode into the camp. Then spring turned to summer, which lasted for about an hour. Mum, Pop, I hate to tell you this: it's the dead of winter now.*

A wave of homesickness hit Alicia. She put down her pen and gazed out the turret window. When her big sister, Lorelei, had come here five years earlier, she had told Alicia that it had mostly been spring and autumn, with only one day of winter in the first session. But she had also said there was "no telling" in a place like Camp Princess.

The young princess sighed. Things like weather never upset Lorelei. She was brave and didn't get homesick. Alicia picked up her pen again and continued writing.

> *So, Mum and Pop, I am including a list of what*
> *I need:*
> * *Silver-fox muff (not the red-fox one; it's not as*
>   *warm)*
> * *Earmuffs (I look stupid in them, but I'll look*
>   *stupider if my ears freeze and drop off.)*
> * *Please, please send me those new-style*
>   *snowshoes with rawhide laces. I want to be*
>   *able to hike over any kind of snow.*
> * *Ice skates—the latest models with the*
>   *unprocessed staghorn blades.*
> * *Also, send my extra pair of high-top,*
>   *fleece-lined suede boots—the purple ones. I'm*
>   *on the Purple team for the Color Wars.*

Alicia paused again in her writing. She wondered if she should tell her parents about the rumors she had overheard about the ghost in the South Turret. Her mother might worry. And her father would call her a "puffball princess." Oh, well, better not mention it, she decided.

Why would a two-hundred-year-old ghost show up now, anyway? She'd certainly be out of fashion! Totally medieval! Alicia thought, trying to make a little joke to set her mind at ease. She went back to her letter.

> *My chambers are all right. I am in the South Turret. I share it with two others, a Princess Gundersnap from Slobodkonia and Princess Kristen, who is from somewhere called the Isles of the Salt Tears in the Realm of Rolm— wherever that is. I heard it's a very wild place. She has the best boots, though!*
>
> *I miss everyone so much. I think of you all having breakfast in the lake pavilion and watching the swans glide over the crystal-blue water. Meanwhile, I'm here snowbound in June in a stone turret! Does that seem quite fair?*

Alicia hastily crossed out the last sentence and wrote, "I'm going to try very hard to get as much as I can out of what Mum calls 'the Camp Princess experience' and give it what Pop calls 'the old camp try.'"

Rah-rah, she thought miserably.

"Well, I shall say good night," she wrote, and then signed the letter.

Yours truly,
Alicia Quintana Mariela Margarita, Princess
of All the Belgravias

P.S. Please be sure to take Gryffie out for a good fly at least twice a week.

P.P.S. Please send me my falconer's glove because someone said the ones here are made of inferior leather.

P.P.P.S. Please don't let little Isabella play with my best jewels.

Chapter 3

TURRETMATES

Alicia put down her quill and slipped the letter into an envelope. She dropped on a blob of wax she had melted over the candle and then pressed her royal seal, a swan with a crown, into the warm wax.

She looked up at the row of gold-braided cords hanging on the wall. Each cord was connected to a different bell in some other part of the castle. She tried to remember which bell would summon the Steward of the Post. She would ask one of her turretmates. She hoped Kristen was there, because she found Gunder-what's-it a little hard to understand.

Alicia walked into the parlor. Shoot! It's Gunderthunder! she thought as she saw the princess sitting in the window seat.

"Pardon me, is Princess Kristen here?" Alicia asked, hoping that she was able to disguise the disappointment in her voice.

"*Nocht,*" the other princess grunted.

Alicia assumed that *nocht* meant "no."

"Well, I have a bit of a problem," she said.

The other princess looked up and blinked.

Oh, dear, thought Alicia, she is rather unfortunate looking, but she has lovely eyes. Sad, though. Does she ever smile?

"Vot is the problem?" Gundersnap said.

"Uh . . . I am not quite sure which cord to pull for the Steward of the Post. I have a letter to send, Princess Gun . . ." Alicia paused.

"Gundersnap," the other princess said and snapped her fingers to illustrate the last part of her name. "It's the third cord from the left."

"Thank you, Princess Gundersnap."

"Come with me. I show you what I did to help."

Alicia followed Gundersnap into her bedchamber. Under each cord, cards in neat writing showed who would be summoned by a pull.

"That's very clever," Alicia said. "Thank you."

"I am not clever. I am practical," Gundersnap replied.

"I think you are clever and practical. You can be both, you know," Alicia said.

Princess Gundersnap chewed on her bottom lip as if she were considering the idea. Alicia looked around the chamber. There were no portraits of Gundersnap's parents, but there was one of a lovely gray pony. "Is that yours?" Alicia asked.

"Yes, yes." Gundersnap smiled, and suddenly her eyes sparkled. "That is my dear, vonderful little Menschmik. He was a birthday present and just a little colt when he was given to me. I have raised and trained him. There has never been a sweeter pony."

Suddenly both girls heard a loud clatter coming from the parlor. The two princesses ran out to see what the noise was. Princess Kristen of the Isles of the Salt Tears in the Realm of Rolm lay on the divan with the thick furs she wore as a cloak. A pair of goggles was perched on top of her head, and under her dress Alicia could see leggings crusted with snow.

"Not a decent iceboat in the fleet!" Kristen groaned.

"Vot?" Gundersnap said.

"A what?" Alicia said at the same moment.

"You don't know what an iceboat is?" Kristen asked.

Alicia and Gundersnap shook their heads.

"Picture a rowboat with sled runners and a sail," Kristen said.

"I can't," Alicia replied.

"I'm trying," Gundersnap said.

"It's like sailing on ice. I won all the races at home. Well, almost all the races," Kristen said.

"Don't your legs get cold out there?" Alicia asked.

"Nope." Kristen pulled her dress higher. "I only wear double-fold cashmere leggings and underwear. None of that lacy stuff."

"Where did you get them?" Alicia asked.

"*L&B* winter catalogue," Kristen said.

"*L&B?*" Alicia asked.

"*Longbow and Blade*, a sports catalogue for knights and squires. It's got mostly weapons, but in the back they have clothing and other gear."

"Oh." Alicia blinked. She read mostly fashion catalogues and magazines. She particularly liked the one called *Classic Crown Jewels*. In the back there were ads for fabulous jewels from kingdoms that had lost all their money and gone broke. Or, as her father would say, had gone "belly up and crown down."

The parlor was filled with a soft tinkling sound. "Enter," the three princesses said in unison. Gilly, the lady's maid, led a small parade into the parlor. She and two other maids each carried an exquisitely beautiful ball gown.

"Time to dress for the Banquet Royale, miladies. It's the first of the camp season and always the fanciest," said Gilly. Kristen groaned.

Behind each maid stood a small boy holding a plump velvet pillow. On top of each pillow was a gold and enamel box that held each princess's jewels, which were normally kept in the royal camp vault. Still smaller boys held other pillows on which their newly shined tiaras perched.

Alicia looked at the tiara on Kristen's pillow. It was made of strange teeth, each tipped with a small but glittering blue sapphire.

"Princess Kristen," Alicia asked, "if I might be so bold, I would like to ask you a question."

"You call asking a question being bold?" The redheaded princess laughed. "Fire away. Ask me anything."

"Well, I notice the teeth in your tiara are the same as the one in your barrette. What kind of animal do they come from?"

"They're from a shark. Great white," Kristen answered.

"A shark!" Alicia and Gundersnap exclaimed. Their

tiaras had diamonds glistening among pearls, with the occasional ruby sprinkled in—although Gundersnap's still resembled a battle helmet more than a tiara.

"By the bones of Saint Michael, how comfortable can a shark-tooth tiara be? I think it would be very scary," Alicia said.

"No, not at all. I'll tell you what is scary—when the shark is alive and staring you in the face. Dead sharks' teeth on my head? No problem."

"You must hurry, miladies," said Gilly, sending the princesses to their chambers to be assisted in dressing by their maids.

"I am to be your maid," Gilly told Alicia as she laid her gown on the bed. "I think that your hair worn up with a curl or two coming down on each side would make the tiara sit ever so prettily on you head. You'll learn all about hair and makeup with the Duchess—"

Gilly's words were cut short by a shriek coming from Kristen's chamber. Alicia and Gilly rushed to the princess's chamber, almost colliding with Gundersnap and Mary, her chambermaid. What had gone wrong?

"It bit me. I swear it bit me!" Annie was crying.

"What are you carrying on about, Annie?" Gilly said firmly.

"It did not bite you!" Kristen said.

"What was it?" Alicia asked. Could a ghost bite? she wondered.

"The princess's tiara, milady. I was trying to arrange it on her head, and she moved. I swear to you it bit me."

"Nonsense!" Gundersnap stepped forward. "The shark is dead. The teeth don't bite without the shark. Now, show me, where did it bite you?"

"There, see." Annie held out her finger. There was a tiny red mark there.

"You probably got that when you pulled your hand away. The rest is your imagination, notting else!" replied Gundersnap. "As Empress Mummy always says, imagination is a waste of time and leads to trouble."

"Thank you, Annie." Kristen stepped between Gundersnap and Annie. "I'll fix my own tiara. I do it all the time at home, anyhow."

"You do?" came a chorus of shocked voices.

"Of course I do. I sail my own boat, I ride my own charger, I shoot my own crossbow. You think I can't put a silly little tiara on my head?"

With that proclamation, Kristen picked up the tiara and jammed it on top of the mass of red curls that Annie had so artfully arranged. They were now all squashed down under the shark-tooth tiara that sat slightly askew on Princess Kristen's head.

Alicia looked around Kristen's chamber. A crossbow hung on the wall. Ribbons from various competitions were suspended from the silk canopy of her bed. A jousting lance was propped in the corner, and she had replaced her dressing table top with a shield that held her combs and brushes. On the walls hung several portraits of her family, a sister and two brothers, all of them with fiery red hair and freckles.

A luxurious animal fur had replaced the plush velvet quilt on her bed. When Kristen noticed Gundersnap looking at it, she said, "I'm allergic to velvet and really prefer to sleep under the skin of animals I have brought down myself."

"What's that one?" Alicia asked, nodding at the bed fur.

"A bear."

"A bear!"

"Yes, he ate my favorite pony."

Gundersnap gasped. "How horrible."

"Terrible!" Kristen said. Her face paled, and her freckles seemed to stand out more. But then she leaped up and slapped the fur. "But he got his!" She gave her tiara a final shove. "Come on, Princesses, let's go!" she whooped, and sailed out of the chamber. Alicia and Gundersnap followed happily, their wide skirts rustling. The maids were left aghast and shaking their heads.

"We have our work cut out for us with that one," Annie said.

"I think perhaps with all of them," Gilly replied.

"You do?" said Mary.

"Yes, I do," Gilly said mysteriously. "But don't get me wrong. I think they are good princesses."

Chapter 4

THE GRAND BANQUET ROYALE

The entire Great Hall was decked out in splendor for the grand Banquet Royale. Candles blazed on tables set with cloths woven with threads of gold and silver. The princesses sparkled like gems in a jewelry box. Their gowns had been embroidered with pounds of pearls and touches of diamonds here and there. Tiaras gleamed as the princesses made their way to the table where their team banners hung.

"It's beautiful!" Princess Alicia exclaimed.

Princess Kristen was squinting and looked slightly annoyed.

"You can hardly see through the glare of the jewels. I

should have worn my sun goggles. There are enough dia-monds around here to skate on."

"Don't tell me you don't like jewels!" Alicia said.

"It's not that I don't like them," Kristen said. "But it's like eating too much candy. Instead of a tummy ache, I am getting an eye ache."

"But what about the ones you're wearing yourself?" asked the tiny Princess Myrella, who sparkled with emeralds. Myrella sat across from Alicia, Gundersnap, and Kristen.

"Sapphires remind me of the blue waters of the Realm of Rolm," Kristen said.

Troubadours strolled through the hall, stopping to sing at each table.

"Oh, I hope they sing about Merlin," Alicia said.

"Merlin?" asked Gundersnap.

"Merlin the magician, the one who protected King Arthur when he was a boy. You haven't heard of him?" Alicia asked.

"*Nocht*," replied Gundersnap. "Magic is not practical, so I would not have heard of him."

"But Merlin could be very practical. Merlin could change Arthur into a fish or bird to teach him lessons for becoming a true king."

"Hmmph," said the Princess of Slobodkonia. "Fish are

to be fried. Did this Merlin give instruction in war craft?"

"War craft?" Alicia looked confused. She had never thought of war as a craft.

A troubadour with a lyre strolled up to their table and began an eerie, mournful song. Alicia felt a chill run along her spine. The song was not about Merlin or Arthur. It was about a ghost.

> *"A spirit floats between the shadows*
> *From ancient times so long ago.*
> *What does she seek? What has she lost?*
> *This weeping ghost, this phantom crossed."*

Could the stories about the ghost be true? Alicia wondered. She'd felt foolish thinking a ghost had caused the scream while they were getting dressed earlier. Still, why did the troubadour come right to the end of the table where the princesses of the South Turret sat? Alicia glanced at Kristen and Gundersnap, but they seemed unconcerned.

When the troubadour had finished his song, Princess Parisiana from the Majestic Realm of Chantillip said, "Now, kind sir, enough about our ghost princess. Have you a song about a cute prince, perhaps one from Camp Burning Shield?"

All the princesses laughed heartily. But a grand lady at

the head of their table, the Duchess of Bagglesnort, who was absolutely encrusted with jewels, gave a disapproving sniff. And in a sharp voice she said, "Such laughing is coarse! Our conversation must be as fine and as sparkling as our jewels."

Silence immediately fell like a thick fog on the table. Alicia stole a glance at the woman and felt a twinge of dislike. She supposed that this duchess was considered beautiful, but to Alicia her face looked like a mask that might crack apart.

Princess Kristen rolled her eyes. The Duchess of Bagglesnort took note.

"Princess Kristen," the duchess said, "you are from the Realm of Rolm, are you not?"

"Yes, Your Grace," Princess Kristen said demurely, and lowered her eyes.

"Would you like to share with us some of your interests from that sea-bound realm? What kind of activities do you enjoy?"

"You mean sports?" Kristen asked.

"If you must. I was thinking more along the lines of art, but yes, sports. What do you like?"

Kristen once more cast her eyes down primly. But Alicia and Gundersnap, who sat on either side of her, could see a sly smile steal across her face.

"I'll tell you what I like. I like a well-rigged sailboat in a thumping gale. I like going fast as a scalded cat down the Channel of Salt Tears, then rounding the mark before my brother, and yelling as I pass him by, 'Suck wind, sucker!'"

The Duchess of Bagglesnort drew out her fan and started to fan herself rapidly. "Smelling salts! Smelling salts!" she cried. A maid ran up with a jeweled vial, uncorked it, and began waving it under the duchess's nose. Meanwhile, the other princesses at the table kept their eyes riveted on Kristen.

"'Suck wind, sucker'? You said that to your brother, a prince?" asked an astonished princess.

"You bet your diamond-splattered bodice!" Kristen shot back with a broad grin.

"Princesses, Princesses!" gasped the Duchess of Bagglesnort. "This conversation is not sparkling."

But it is, thought Alicia as they began to eat. Although she would never use such language herself, she was secretly thrilled by her new friend's boldness. How glad she was that Kristen was her turretmate!

After dinner a trumpet blew a fanfare. The Queen Mum stood up from her throne at the far end of the longest banquet table, where the third-year princesses sat. The Camp Mistress was even taller than Alicia remembered. A large powdered wig with puffs of hair piled up on her head like towering clouds added to her height. "Welcome, Princesses, to our first official banquet of the camp season. You know your teams for the Color Wars. There shall be exciting contests and competitions throughout our first two-week session and in each of the sessions thereafter. The winning team shall be celebrated in song and dance and even embroidery. Your accomplishments and triumphs shall be stitched into the camp tapestry. You, campers, shall stitch one panel during needlepoint for each session under the superb guidance of our needlepoint counselor, Lady Merry von Schleppenspiel."

"Needlepoint?" whispered Kristen to Gundersnap. "Why not a nice big trophy for the winner?"

"Yes, a trophy, much more practical, I think," Gundersnap added.

"If the weather cooperates," the Camp Mistress continued, "one of our biggest activities for this session shall be songbird catching in the Forest of Chimes. Autumn is the best time to catch these lovely creatures. So as soon as the first leaf turns, all new princesses will dash out to find a bird. And when you catch one, you shall begin training it. Remember, the songbird contest is the most important event of the first session's Color Wars. It is our belief here at Camp Princess that if one can teach a songbird to sing beautifully, one can lead a nation. Remember, Princesses, you were born to rule!"

Gundersnap whispered, "'Born to rule.' I like that!"

The tiny Princess Myrella leaned forward. "My cousin from the Kingdom of Blitzen was camp champion in the songbird contest for three years running," she said.

"Is she here this year?" Kristen asked.

"Oh, no. She's preparing for her wedding. She is to marry the King of Glenbyrren."

Gundersnap whispered in Alicia's ear, "A puppet king. My mother invaded that country two years ago. She really runs the place."

"Oh!" Alicia said quietly. She was not sure if she would really like Gundersnap's mother, Maria Theresa, Empress of All the Slobodks.

The Queen Mum was saying, "Tonight after dinner the Third Years shall give a concert for us in the Hall of Music with their birds—birds they found in their first year. You shall be amazed how well the Third Years have taught their birds to sing. And soon you too shall be as skillful in teaching your songbirds.

"But now for dessert." The Queen Mum raised a long white hand in the air and snapped her fingers. Attendants extinguished the largest candles. A long "aaah" and gasps of amazement followed as two lines of footmen entered. Each one held an elaborate fantasy of spun-sugar cakes and molded ice creams. Set atop these delectable structures were sparkler wands fizzing with light.

"It's the *Great Ship Maude*! How totally ice!" exclaimed Kristen as a dessert was set before her. This was apparently a Sea of Salt Tears expression.

"It's Heart's Purr," said Myrella as another footman gave her a spun-sugar castle. The castle appeared to float on a pond with water lilies made of frosting.

"The Belgravian Gardens," Alicia said as a wave of homesickness overcame her. "The swans are so lovely."

"And the fourteenth regiment of the Grand Grenadiers. Oh, look, even little cannons! It's the battle of Pliny Field. Very important." Gundersnap bent forward to examine her dessert. "Ooh, the cavalry looks yummy!"

"Who wants a sail? I think they're made of marzipan," Kristen said as she dismantled the *Great Ship Maude* by pulling out its chocolate mast.

"Why was that particular battle so important, Princess Gundersnap?" Alicia asked.

"A very savage king was defeated. He enslaved all the people. Even children were forced to work for notting, and the whipping boy's family received no pay."

"Whipping boy!" Kristen almost shrieked. "Hello! That went out a couple of centuries ago."

Alicia turned to Gundersnap. "Do any royal households still employ whipping boys? It's so . . . so . . . so Dark Ages."

But Gundersnap had turned quite red. "Well, I think it has, for the most part."

Alicia had the most dreadful feeling that perhaps the Empress of All the Slobodks still employed a whipping boy to receive the beatings for the small crimes and mistakes of any royal child. She knew that Gundersnap had fifteen brothers and sisters, so they probably had to have at least two or three whipping boys. The more Alicia heard about the Empress Maria Theresa, the less she liked about her.

After dessert the princesses followed the Queen Mum to the Hall of Music. The third-year princesses sat on a stage, each with a caged bird on her lap. The first to perform was Princess Kinna from the Queendom of Mattunga, a beautiful princess with skin the color of dark cinnamon. She wore her hair in a cascade of hundreds of braids.

"How many braids do you think she's wearing?" Kristen whispered.

"One hundred forty-eight," Princess Rosamunde answered. "It's the fashion in the Queendom of Mattunga."

"Queendom?" Alicia asked.

"Yes, only women are allowed to rule."

Princess Kinna took her bird from its cage. She gave the bird a small signal and it opened its beak. A long stream of notes poured forth. At certain points Princess Kinna joined the bird in song.

It was a stunning performance. Alicia gasped as the music ended. Yes, indeed, if one could lead a songbird to sing so beautifully, one could lead a nation to greatness, Alicia thought proudly. There was loud applause.

"Inspiring!" the Queen Mum exclaimed. Onstage she congratulated Princess Kinna. Then she turned to the audience. "It can be done, miladies. It can be done!"

But Alicia was worried. She was good at a lot of things, and she was musical, but could she do this? The idea of the contest being so important made her nervous. Very nervous.

That evening Alicia felt a chill in her room that added to her unease. She lit her special reading candle. It had a small hood so no one could see the light from under her door.

She snuggled beneath her velvet blankets and ran her hand lightly over her book's tattered cover, embossed with gold scrolling that had long ago lost its gleam. She opened the book, read a few lines, and sighed with utter delight. Yet she was still mystified. Why had these two lovers been separated?

Their love was so deep it was almost painful. The Forgotten Princess enchanted Alicia, and she read a few more lines before her eyes began to close. Suddenly worn out by all of the evening's excitement, she tucked the book under her pillows and fell deeply asleep.

From the window, a sliver of moonlight stole across her face as the clock began to chime midnight, and something cold brushed against her cheek. Someone seemed to whisper into her dreams, "There is more to my story. You must help. . . ."

By morning she had forgotten the words, forgotten even her dreams. But still she had awakened with the odd feeling that there had been a presence, or perhaps a visitation, as she slept.

Chapter 5

A MYSTERY IN STITCHES

Princesses always had breakfast in bed. It was a custom in most kingdoms to avoid "the morning's royal crankies." But the crankies returned in full force when Kristen and Gundersnap were informed by Gilly that their first activity would be needlepoint.

"Borrrrring!" said Princess Kristen.

"Vee haven't von anyting yet!" said Princess Gundersnap. "Vot is there to stitch about?"

Alicia simply yawned. It was still winter, and she was feeling lazy. As much as she loved to embroider, she would much rather curl up with her book and sip hot chocolate with lots of whipped cream by a cozy fire.

But off to needlepoint they went.

"Gently, gently, Princess Kristen. You're not on a hunt heaving a spear into a wild boar. This is needlework." There were muffled giggles from all of the princesses who sat at the large embroidery frame as they began to stitch the background for the camp tapestry.

The needlepoint counselor, Lady Merry von Schleppenspiel, was an enormous lady. She did not simply have double chins, but quadruple, quintuple, octogubble chins.

Alicia silently counted them as she stole glances from the portion of the panel she had been assigned to work on. There were indeed eight chins. The woman was of enormous girth, and the seams of her sea-blue silk dress appeared ready to split. Her fingers looked like sausages. Her feet poked out under the ruffled hem of her dress. They were tiny but oozed out over the edges of her shoes.

Alicia frowned at her work. She was proud that Lady von Schleppenspiel thought she was ready for the complicated split stitch, which was usually left for the third-year princesses. But it was very difficult. She had had to pick out the threads from the feather of a bird in the Forest of Chimes three times now.

"Princess Kristen, I gave you the snow daisies. Those are easy. It's a straight simple stitch," Lady von Schleppenspiel said gently.

"Maybe for you, Lady von Schleppenspiel. But my hands are accustomed to holding an oar or a jousting lance," Kristen replied. Then under her breath she added, "This sucks!"

There was a wave of tittering from the other princesses. "Yes," Kristen continued. "In the Realm of Rolm, girls *can* joust. They *can* also sail boats and ride on boar hunts if they are so inclined. And I am. I don't give a pinch for the needle arts and all that. Give me a lance, a spear, or a sword. Those are my needles!"

"Well, my dear." Lady von Schleppenspiel cocked her head so that several of her chins seemed to slide off to one side. "If you don't finish the tapestry, it shall never be displayed, and since I am the needlepoint counselor, it is my job to see that it is completed. Just look around you when you walk through the castle and you will see our camp history. All the tapestries for all the hundreds of years of Camp Princess have been finished." Lady von Schleppenspiel paused for effect. "All except one, that is."

"Why wasn't it finished?" asked Alicia, suddenly interested.

"Oh, if it's true, it's rather a sad story."

"Do tell us, please!" Princess Gundersnap asked in a pleading voice.

"Yes, do!" said Princess Kinna.

"Princess Kinna of the Queendom of Mattunga, you as a Third Year have heard this story many times, I would imagine."

"Yes, but it is a lovely story, Lady von Schleppenspiel."

"It is a story as unfinished as the tapestry," replied Lady Merry.

"Go on!" the other princesses urged.

"Well . . ." Lady von Schleppenspiel sighed. "It was said that more than a century ago, a princess with a broken heart took refuge here. No one knows why her heart was broken or why she came to Camp Princess. Some say that she had been a camper here in her youth. In any case, when she returned she became the needlepoint counselor. Her stitches were supposedly magnificent—tiny, tight, and they gleamed. But she never laughed or smiled, and she hardly ever ate. She wasted away until finally she died of a broken heart."

A hush fell over the room. Needles stopped moving, and sighs could be heard coming from more than a few princesses.

Lady von Schleppenspiel broke the silence.

"The oddest part," she continued, "is that year's tapestry

vanished. It simply disappeared within an hour of the princess's death."

"Was it stolen?" Princess Gundersnap asked.

"Why would anyone steal an unfinished tapestry?" Princess Kristen asked.

Yes, thought Alicia. Why would anyone steal an unfinished tapestry, unless they did not want the rest of the story to be finished and therefore known? This was a true mystery. Alicia's mind wandered as she continued stitching.

When the needlepoint hour had ended, the princesses of the South Turret found themselves together in one of the many winding corridors of the castle. Princess Myrella tagged along with the group shyly. Except for Alicia, everyone was jabbering about how they thought camp was supposed to be fun but so far the most fun part had been the spectacular desserts of the night before.

"What happened to archery?" asked Kristen.

"Any pony riding?" asked Gundersnap.

"And swimming!" Myrella said. "They might think I am just a fraction of a princess in size, but I bet that I can beat any princess in this camp in a swimming race."

"You can?" Kristen asked.

"I think so."

"Great. Let's make a bet." They paused on the steps to

seal their bet with the traditional Royal Princess Oath for competitions. Touching their everyday tiaras, they both recited the words.

"Cross my crown and hope to die
If in this contest I deny
My rightful place as first in sport,
And may the loser grow a wart!"

It was a nonsensical little ditty. No one had ever died by losing this kind of competition, nor had anyone grown a wart. But it was still fun and considered good sportsmanship to say the pledge.

"You know," said Alicia thoughtfully, "this needlepoint thing is not as boring as you all seem to think."

"Why not?" asked Kristen.

"Because it's a mystery." The other three princesses' eyes brightened as Alicia went on. "We could solve it. A tapestry cannot simply disappear into thin air. This is a big castle. It must be here somewhere."

"But vhere should vee begin looking?" Princess Gundersnap said.

"And how?" asked Princess Myrella.

"And we must keep it a secret," said Kristen. "We don't

want everyone looking for it."

"Yes," said Alicia. Then she turned to Princess Myrella. "Princess Myrella, you must not breathe a word of this to your turretmates."

"Oh, don't worry. They hardly speak to me," the small princess said sadly.

"They don't? Vhy not?" Gundersnap asked.

"I don't know. I'm small, easily overlooked. And they are very snooty, for the most part. They think I come from a swamp. That's what they call the Marsh Kingdoms. Princess Zelenka asked to see my feet. She said she had heard a rumor that they were webbed. And Princess Millicent is just so boastful because her father invaded the Fresnian Islands."

"*Acht!*" Princess Gundersnap made a scalding sound in the back of her throat. "Those islands are notting. Empress Mummy wouldn't touch them with a ten-foot cannon. No natural resources, bugs all over the place, half an island gets washed away every year. Notting to brag about, believe me."

"Who's your fourth turretmate?"

Myrella made a terrible face. "She is the worst of all. Princess Morwenna. All she does is pray. She does not permit laughter in her presence. And her favorite saint is Saint Rumwald."

"Rumwald!" exclaimed Alicia. "The baby saint?"

Myrella nodded.

"That is the saddest saint in Christendom," Kristen said. "He died when he was just three days old."

"So you can see," Myrella continued, "I wouldn't exactly be telling these turretmates much. And then they are all Crimsons, and I am a Purple."

"How did that happen?" Alicia asked. "I thought turretmates were all members of the same team."

"Maybe if you're one-third a princess, they think you're not quite Purple or Crimson, just some color in between," Myrella said sadly.

"Maybe you could change turrets," Kristen said.

"It's against the rules," Gundersnap said. "Rule three, section two, article one says, 'No princess is permitted to request a turret change during a session. A request may be made for the next session, but it is rarely granted.'"

"You've read all the rules?" Alicia asked.

"And memorized them. Empress Mummy will be quizzing me on them in her letters."

"Rules are made to be broken!" Kristen said. "Look, Myrella. You're little—a one-third princess—but look at the upside. That's a special circumstance. It means you should be able to fit in anywhere."

"Well, I guess it's worth a try," said Myrella. "It's very nice of you. I'd much rather have you as turretmates than them."

"I'll get right on it," said Gundersnap. "Draft a proposal."

The other three princesses blinked at one another. Princess Gundersnap was all business. There was no denying that.

"And I," Alicia said, "shall put on my thinking tiara to figure out where this tapestry might be."

"You have a thinking tiara?" Myrella asked.

"Yes, pure silver, but quite plain with no diamonds. Lightweight, fits any hairstyle, simple but elegant, no distractions. I can concentrate quite well in it. It's been in the family for years."

"Not from Batwhistle, the pawnbrokers?" asked Myrella.

"No. All our tiaras are heirlooms. It's really the best way, Mum says."

"Very practical," said Gundersnap. "I would no more wear another family's tiara than swap underclothes with them."

"Eeeew!" All four princesses wrinkled up their noses in disgust, and then they all burst out laughing.

Chapter 6

PRAYERS AND WHISPERS

When the three princesses returned to the South Turret that night, Gilly and the other maids were waiting for them with their freshly pressed nightclothes. They also handed each girl a scroll with the activities list for the next day.

Alicia unrolled hers and glanced at it with a frown. "A swim test?" she said. "What's that?"

"Swim test, weather permitting," Gilly corrected. She looked out the window at the swirling snow.

"But I don't know how to swim," Alicia said.

"*Nocht*, me neither. Can't swim," Princess Gundersnap added.

"Don't know how to swim?" Princess Kristen looked up

from her activity scroll. "Amazing! I could swim before I could walk. All children in the Realm of Rolm know how to swim."

"Then you shall probably be put in the advanced group that goes to the lake outside the castle walls and not the moat," Gilly told her.

"Moat?" Princess Alicia said in alarm. "Is it clean? Sanitary? I don't want to come down with anything."

"What about crocodiles? We have crocodiles in our moat at home," Princess Gundersnap said.

"Oh, how horrible," Alicia said. Another one of the empress's ideas, no doubt! she added silently.

"Don't worry, milady," reassured Gilly gently. "We have no crocodiles, and we have the cleanest waters in all the kingdom."

"Makeup!" Kristen suddenly roared, looking at the list. "What's this about makeup? I don't wear makeup! What would I need with rouge?" Indeed, the Princess of the Isles of the Salt Tears seemed rather violently pink in the cheeks.

"If I may be permitted, Princess Kristen, I think you will find the Duchess of Bagglesnort very informative," Gilly said. "She is considered a great beauty, and her knowledge of cosmetics is quite profound."

"How profound can makeup be?" Kristen scowled.

Alicia and Gundersnap looked at each other and began to giggle.

Gilly herself suppressed a smile, but she knew she simply could not laugh in front of the princesses. It would be grounds for dismissal if she were discovered laughing at the expense of one of the counselors, especially the Duchess of Bagglesnort, who was a very mean-spirited lady. If Gilly were to laugh and it got back to the duchess, she would not be acting like a proper lady's maid and would have to pack her belongings and hit the road.

"Well, it's time for your nightly prayers and then to bed, miladies," she said. "Tomorrow is going to be an exciting day at camp. You'll need all your energy."

"For makeup?" Kristen muttered under her breath.

"For swimming?" Alicia said anxiously.

"Well, possibly for chasing after songbirds in the Forest of Chimes—if it is an autumn day," Gilly told them.

Each princess bade the others good night and then knelt in prayer by her bedside.

Kristen prayed for an iceboat, "especially, dear Lord, if winter stays."

Alicia prayed that it would continue to be winter for just a little while, so she would not have to take her swim test. "Oh, dear Lord. I'm a little bit homesick. I miss Mum and Pop so much, and I really don't want to swim in a moat. It sounds so . . . so . . . icky."

And Gundersnap prayed for a dwarf and a pony. "Please,

dear God, make Gortle's headaches go away and his poor bent legs not pain him. And make Mummy not call on him to dance and tumble for the amusement of the court. Watch out for dear Gortle, God, and for my dear pony, Menschmik." And then she had another thought. "Oh, and P.S., dear Lord, may I not drown in the moat."

As the last candle was snuffed out, a lovely sound swelled through the castle. It was the Royal Camp Choir accompanied by their songbirds. As the third-year girls made their way through the long corridors and twisting passages of Camp Princess, they sang the sweet and slightly mournful song known as "The Princess Taps."

> *"Day is done, gone the sun*
> *From the hills, from the lake,*
> *From the sky*
> *And towers high.*
> *The stars in heaven's gown*
> *Bright as jewels in thy crown.*
>
> *But rest ye now, Princesses royal.*
> *Dream of thrones*
> *But keep ye loyal*
> *To your people*
> *And your kingdoms,*

Safe they keep
While you sleep."

Alicia couldn't fall asleep, so she decided to read another letter or two from *Love Letters of a Forgotten Princess*. Yes, these were the letters of an aching heart, she thought as she lit her special reading candle. Would anybody ever ache for her as the princess ached for her true love? Or would she ever feel such a yearning for a true love?

Her own parents had a very happy marriage, but it wasn't this romantic, Alicia thought wistfully. She didn't wish her mum and pop pain, but just a little achy romance would be awfully interesting. Not heartbreak-achy, not like the poor needlepoint counselor who died of a broken heart before the tapestry was finished. That would be like so, well, over the top.

She remembered that she wanted to put on her thinking tiara and figure out what was with this tapestry. She scrambled out of bed and got the tiara from its velvet box. Then she climbed back under the covers and, with her thinking tiara firmly in place, Alicia thought about where the ancient tapestry might be hidden. She wracked her brain, but nothing came. Instead, the open page of her book caught her eye. It was one of her favorite letters.

. . . and so, My True Love, evil cannot part
us, neither the Blood Guard nor the treacherous
queen. We shall meet in another world, a better
world. A world that has neither kings, nor
queens, nor princes or princesses. A world
without crowns, but one where we shall be
clad only in the light of the stars that shine
through us.

This was the part that always confused Alicia. Was the forgotten princess talking about being dead? Dead and stark naked in heaven? That is what it sounded like to Alicia, but she never dared ask what it might really mean.

As the candle sputtered out, Alicia drifted off to sleep. The thinking tiara slipped off her head and onto the pillow. A chill filled the air and Alicia shivered, pulling her velvet covers up under her chin.

Something cold brushed her cheek just as she fell asleep. And once again a voice whispered, "Young princess, I am old. Please help—not all my tale is told."

But once again, by morning she had forgotten the words, forgotten even the whisper in her dreams. Yet still there was that strange sensation that someone, something had passed through her chamber as she slept.

Chapter 7

AN AMPLE LADY

The next morning the three princesses of the South Turret emerged from their bedchambers in their best winter clothes. They were struck by an amazing sight.

"*Munk doctum!*" gasped Gundersnap in Slobo.

"Holy halibut!" whispered Kristen.

"Lady von Schleppenspiel!" Alicia exclaimed.

The needlepoint counselor sat in a very large rocking chair, dozing. The girls' exclamations had not sent even the faintest ripple across the placid lake of sleep in which she seemed to be completely immersed.

Suddenly a strange noise rumbled up from Lady Merry's massive body. The silk that spanned her stomach gave a lurch. Her mouth opened and a very large burp came out, causing a chandelier overhead to shudder.

The lady's eyes flew open. "Oh, my goodness! My goodness! You're here! Oh, miladies, shame on me for drifting off like this. And here I am awakened by my own digestive music. I'm afraid I sounded very much like the tuba in a marching band—my gut, that is!" She giggled. It was a teeny-weeny little giggle, which seemed odd to Alicia, coming from an enormous woman who had just burped loud enough to shake a chandelier.

Princess Gundersnap stepped forward. "Vye are you here, please?"

"Oh, my goodness." The lady began chuckling. "They didn't tell you? I am not just your needlepoint counselor; I am your lady-in-waiting. I know von Schleppenspiel is quite a mouthful. My full name is Lady Merry von Schlepp . . . etcetera, etcetera." She waved her hand dismissively. "You know the rest. You may call me simply Lady Merry, as in Merry Christmas. Princesses are permitted to call their ladies-in-waiting by their first names as long as that name is preceded by the correct title. Rule two, section four, article five of the rule book."

"B-b-but," stammered Alicia. "I thought we were each to have our own lady-in-waiting."

"Oh, there's a shortage this year, and I do believe I am

ample enough for three. One of me equals three ladies-in-waiting. Wouldn't you agree?" Lady Merry asked. And now she started laughing quite hard again.

The three princesses stood transfixed as the guffaws set the eight chins rippling. The ripples traveled through Lady Merry's body until her midsection jiggled. Her tiny feet were caught in an antic dance of their own as she kicked them out from the hem of her gown. She reminded the princesses of a ship caught in the midst of a violent squall. These were no longer simply ripples. These were waves, and the princesses watched closely to see if the vessel itself would hold. Would the seams split? Alicia wondered.

Finally the laughter subsided, and Lady Merry whisked a dainty hanky from somewhere deep in the bodice of her dress and wiped the tears from her eyes.

"Yes, miladies, I must tell you that I do prefer the word 'ample' to 'fat.' 'Fat' just sounds too dense to me. Ample, amplitude—a lady of great amplitude—yes, rather nice, I think. Or a lady of ample proportions suggests that I am much more than just fat—I have room for many things. By that I mean more things than just the common ones such as etiquette lessons. That is the standard stuff we ladies-in-waiting are expected to help you learn." She daintily put the hanky to her mouth and burped again, though not as loudly as she had before.

"For example, muffling a belch. I can do it even better than that when pressed." She held up a hand and waved her sausagelike fingers for silence. "Listen!" Once more she raised the hanky to her mouth. The princesses saw a tremor pass through the sea-blue bodice of the dress, but they heard nothing.

"Totally fab!" Kristen said.

"We shall have burping contests! We'll see who does the best. Oh, miladies, we're going to have such fun! Now, it is suddenly spring, I see. So how about we all go out and play a bit of lawn tennis?"

"You play lawn tennis?" Alicia asked.

"Of course!" Lady Merry exclaimed. "I play it sitting down. I have discovered that almost everything one does standing up can be done sitting down. Ring for my servants, please, and then we'll be off."

Before the servants had arrived, the soft green of the new spring leaves had begun to darken. "Hold it!" Lady Merry raised her hand for silence and stared out the window. "My goodness, miladies, regard the leaves of spring." She paused. "As they darken to the deep green of summer and . . . and . . ." Lady Merry squealed with delight. "The first orange leaf of autumn is here. We all know what that means—we must go to the Forest of Chimes."

"What?" Kristen said. "A two-minute summer? Total weirdness."

The girls were having trouble following Lady Merry and keeping up with the ever-changing seasons.

"Quickly now, we must get out bird-catching nets. This is the songbirds' hour," Lady Merry said.

"Or minute?" Alicia asked.

"Would it not be more practical to vait?" said Gundersnap.

"No, my dear, nothing is practical here. Not at Camp Princess! Oh, practical! What an odd little word!" Lady Merry seemed quite amused. "And furthermore, when autumn happens like this, it always stays for at least a day."

Let's hope so, Alicia thought. She feared it might take her a day to capture a songbird. She was getting even more nervous about the songbird contest.

Chapter 8

THE FOREST OF CHIMES

The Forest of Chimes was indeed a most enchanting place. It was a place of music. The songs of the birds mingled with the chimes of the trees, which had bells on them instead of leaves.

Alicia had been following a little golden bird through the forest, but just as she swooped the net down, the bird escaped. She paused now to catch her breath and listen. It was a most musical forest. Even the stream that ran through the forest did not simply gurgle, but poured forth a song of liquid silvery notes like those plucked from the strings of a harp.

In the distance she could hear cries of delight as other princesses caught their birds. But just as Alicia had feared, she was having no luck at all. She peeked into a rotted-out tree stump filled with moss. It was said that sometimes birds hid in mossy places. But Alicia saw nothing inside except a few spiders.

Not far away, Alicia spotted a lovely tree with low-hanging branches. She could almost touch the bells as she stood beneath them. She looked up and searched for birds that might be hiding among the bells. But all she saw were the crystal clappers that made the beautiful sounds.

"Alicia! Time to come in, dear," Lady Merry called. "Don't worry if you don't catch your songbird today. There is always tomorrow."

But tomorrow won't be the same, Alicia thought sadly as she walked back toward the edge of the forest. It might be winter again, or maybe even a hot summer day when the birds were said to be too tired to sing. And even now the light was growing dim. It would be harder to find a bird as the sun sank toward the horizon and twilight set in.

Alicia turned her head quickly as she heard the tiniest tinkling chimes of a bell bush. She saw a flash of gold. A bird had settled in the thickest part of the bush.

Alicia tiptoed toward the sound. Never mind the net,

she thought. Her hand darted out and she caught the song-bird in her hands. The songbird was hers! It was a beauty—a deep golden color with lovely turquoise flecks sprinkled on its wings.

Twilight was deepening as Alicia began to find her way out of the forest. In the fading light, she had the oddest sensation that someone was following her. It could hardly be Lady Merry. Trees would be crashing and the earth underfoot quaking, she thought, trying to distract herself with this silly thought. Twice she looked behind her to see if there was something. But she saw nothing unusual. Still, she could not shake the eerie sense of being followed. Finally she emerged from the forest.

Lady Merry was fretting when Alicia reached her. "I was about to send in the game warden to find you. You had me worried to death, my dear. How would it look if I lost you on my first day as your lady-in-waiting? I have never lost a princess in all my years here. And I don't intend to."

Alicia followed the sedan chair in which Lady Merry rode, carried by two footmen. For the walk back to the castle, the ample lady muttered about naughty, headstrong princesses. "Naughty, naughty princesses, one in every lot. I'm older now. Don't know if I can still take it."

But Lady Merry did take time to examine the bird Alicia

had caught and pronounced it enchanting. "He's simply enchanting. And it's a weeb—how lucky!"

"What's a weeb?" Alicia asked.

"A weeb, my dear, is a lovely bird found only in the Forest of Chimes. He is very rare indeed."

"How can you tell it's a he?" Alicia asked.

"Do you see the bright turquoise spots on the wings?" Lady Merry said as she gently stroked the bird's feathers. "That is how one tells with weebs. The females don't have those spots. And it's said males are very difficult to teach. But when they finally learn, they have voices beyond compare. They are dear, sweet little birds."

"Will you sing me a nice tune and then let me teach you more, dear, sweet little bird?" Alicia asked.

The little bird seemed to shake his head. He looked at her as if he wanted or needed something. Alicia felt a cold shiver run up her spine.

When she returned to the South Turret, Alicia heard her two turretmates already practicing with their songbirds in the parlor.

"Listen up, birdie boy, I'll sing you a sea shanty," Kristen was saying.

"*Nocht, nocht, nocht*, Princess Kristen. That is much too difficult for a beginning piece. You must try something with a good, precise beat. Vatch me!" Princess Gundersnap had an orange and green bird perched on her finger. She now stretched her arm straight out in front of her. "*Vrachtun*, birdie," she said firmly. Alicia thought that this must be the call for attention in Slobo.

Gundersnap gave the bird a crisp salute with her free hand.

"Holy monk bones! He's saluting her back," Alicia gasped.

"Totally ice!" exclaimed Kristen.

Indeed, the bird had raised one wing slightly in what could only be thought of as a birdlike salute. Then Gundersnap began marching around the salon of the turret.

"Hup, two, three, four. Hup, two, three, four. Sound off, tweet tweet!"

The bird tweet tweeted back! "Hup, two, three, four. Hup, two, three, four," Gundersnap sang happily.

"That's not a real song, Princess Gundersnap," Kristen said.

"Of course not. It is the first drill exercise of the Empress's Grenadiers."

Alicia herself could hardly wait to get started, but there would be no military exercises for her beautiful bird. She went into her own chamber, put her bird into the cage hanging by the window, and got out the book that had been distributed to all the princesses, *Basic Songbird Instruction*.

"'Lesson one,'" she read. She tapped on the cage lightly with her finger. "'Training a songbird always begins with scales,'" she continued. Then she sang, "Do, re, mi, fa, so, la, ti, do!"

The little bird tilted his head slightly as if he were listening to Alicia, but he remained silent. Alicia tried again. She sang each note of the scale slowly and clearly, waiting between each note to let the bird join in. Nothing. She tried one more time, but the weeb simply sat in his cage and stared at her.

"Oh, dear, I hope I don't have a dud of a songbird!" Alicia murmured.

As she spoke, the shutters shook violently and swung open. A blast of raw, cold air came rushing in. The golden weeb started beating his wings against the walls of his cage as the wind swirled around Alicia. Then the wind and the weeb grew calm.

"What was that all about?" Alicia whispered, terrified, as she closed the shutters. The South Turret was beginning to feel creepier and creepier!

That night in bed, long after she had said her prayers and read two long letters from the Forgotten Princess, Alicia tried to sleep but only tossed and turned. Although her little bird remained silent and hardly fluttered a feather, Alicia seemed to feel another presence in the room. It was still autumn, but she felt so cold it could have been winter. Alicia remembered her own little joke about a two-hundred-year-old ghost being quite out of fashion. It didn't seem so funny now. Gundersnap and Kristen were both much braver than she was. Alicia wished she could run to them now. But she did not want to be what her father called a puffball princess. Her pop's words came back to her: "You know, dear Alicia, being a princess has its responsibilities. One must be firm and fair in judgment. One must be steadfast, true to one's beliefs, and brave in the face of danger."

"I don't believe in ghosts!" Alicia whispered in the firmest voice she could.

Her father would say, "Don't be one of those puffball princesses like Aunt Molly, always dithering about. Despite her pretty ways, she has about as much sense as a chicken. Exactly like a Belgravian Meadow Hen—all pretty feathers but not much else, and scared of its own shadow."

The flames of the fire in the grate cast shadows across the floor of Alicia's chamber. Alicia dared herself to sit straight up in bed and watch her own shadow for at least ten seconds. "One . . . two . . . three. . . ," she counted. As she moved her head, she saw her shadow with its loosed hair spread upward on the wall. She raised her arms. "Five . . . six . . . seven." She felt the bird staring at her. "Well, go ahead and stare!" she muttered. "Eight . . . nine . . . ten." She'd done it. "I am not a puffball princess!" she said in a firm voice—and then dived under her velvet blankets, pulling them up around her head.

When the clock chimed midnight, she was still not asleep. So Alicia decided to read just a few more pages.

> *Dearest, I must flee, I must flee, for your safety as well as mine. We must be apart if we shall ever have any hope of being together. I shall return to the place where I was happiest before I met you. Though I have no hope of throne or kingdom, I will be taken in and made welcome.*

Alicia had often wondered what that happy place was. Where was it? What made the Forgotten Princess so happy? It must be a lovely place, she was sure. Each time she read this passage, Alicia wished that she could go to that place where her heroine sought refuge. If only she had been born back then, she could have helped the Forgotten Princess. How ice would that be? Alicia loved Kristen's odd expressions. Yes, totally ice to help the Forgotten Princess.

As she read, she grew drowsy, and the book soon fell to her chest. Her hands rested on the cover. Did she feel the beating of her own heart through its well-worn pages? Or were there two hearts beating? And did she hear the dim notes of a song that a bird could be singing? Or was it part of a dream?

Chapter 9

THE DUCHESS OF BAGGLESNORT
AND OTHER ANNOYANCES

"So you see, Your Highnesses, you cannot entrust the delicate application of these powders to your maids."

The Duchess of Bagglesnort narrowed her eyes and surveyed the roomful of young princesses. "Prepare yourself for a shock." She turned toward the door.

A very elderly woman dressed all in black lace was carried in on a sedan chair. "Lift your veil, Countess Vinky," the duchess said.

Two withered hands shaking with age began to lift the veil. "Holy monk bones!" whispered Alicia. The gasps of fifteen princesses swirled through the air. The countess's face was gray and shriveled, and one side drooped.

"Speak!" commanded the duchess.

The countess struggled to open her mouth, and when she did the words slid out one side in a slur. "The damage to my face is the result of a mixture of white lead and vinegar. I would strongly advise against using these ingredients."

Each girl in the room began to tremble, picturing her own face shriveled, scaly, and drooping to one side.

"Thank you, Countess," the duchess said. "Take her away." She waved her hand in a dismissive gesture.

Alicia looked at Kristen. "Mean!" She mouthed the word. Kristen nodded. Then they both heard Gundersnap whisper, "I do not like this duchess."

"Now, please notice my complexion." The duchess gently touched her face with long, tapering fingers. "It is as clear and white as the finest china. My skin is like porcelain, as many of my suitors have said!" The duchess's lips coiled up into a smug little smile that reminded Alicia of two worms snuggling. "A bit of talc, ground chalk, and egg whites. That is the secret recipe."

The duchess walked among the princesses, who sat at long tables as an assistant distributed the ingredients they were to pound and mix in their stone bowls. She stopped when she came to Kristen and put her hands to the princess's face.

"Oh, dear, I should have noticed this the first night at the banquet. A flame child."

"A what?" Kristen asked.

"You flare, dear, you flare. You must use extra talc to calm down the coloring. My goodness, young lady, you're turning redder and redder."

Kristen's eyes were flashing now, and Alicia thought she actually might explode.

"I am what I am," Kristen said through gritted teeth.

"I think she's rather pretty, milady," Princess Myrella said. "Brown hair, blond hair, black hair, that's so ordinary."

Wrong thing to say, Myrella, Alicia thought. But it was too late. The Duchess of Bagglesnort wheeled around. "There is no such thing as ordinary hair, just ordinary princesses—like yourself, little one, oozing out of the Marsh Kingdoms. What a mistake it was to admit you to Camp Princess."

Gundersnap, Alicia, and Kristen were shocked beyond belief. They had never heard a royal person addressed so rudely. Poor little Myrella already had tears running down her face.

Princess Kinna leaned over and put her arm around her. "Don't worry, little princess. She's like that. When she saw me with my dark cinnamon skin, she said all sorts of rude things. She loves having someone to pick on. Don't pay any attention to her." Then in a lower voice she whispered, "She is very ordinary herself. There are rumors that she bought her title."

"Really!" Myrella looked up with her deep-green eyes.

Princess Kinna nodded and smiled.

"Oh, dear, dear, dear!" The duchess had moved on and was making clicking sounds with her tongue. "What have we here!"

"Vee have me, Princess Gundersnap, of the Empire of Slobodkonia."

"How oddly you speak! It is "we" with a *W*, not *V*. Your pasty complexion and those blemishes are bad enough without that accent. We must send you to the speech counselor."

Alicia and Kristen exchanged looks. How would they ever survive this class? If only it would stop raining, they might get to do something fun outdoors.

But the makeup class went on and on and on. The princesses learned how to grind rouge from rose petals and red clay and to make their eyebrows darker with charcoal and lighter with paste. They were excited to learn a remedy for pimples, but it turned out to be so dreadful that no one had the nerve to try it. It consisted of squished snails mixed with salt and applied directly to the skin. They were also given instruction in the proper placement of beauty marks.

"Not on the end of your nose, Princess Kristen!" the duchess roared. The princess simply smiled at her sweetly and said, "Look, Duchess, no hands!" She crossed her eyes and tried to take the beauty mark off with the tip of her tongue. The Duchess of Bagglesnort was not amused.

"Look!" said Princess Kinna, pointing to the window. "It's stopped raining and it's summer again!"

The golden leaves of autumn had once more turned the lush green of deep summer. Sunlight streamed into the room, and two butterflies with gold wings sported in spiraling flights outside a window. Carpets of wildflowers spread their gay colors across the grass.

"Swimming!" someone cried out.

The good news for Alicia was that makeup was over. The bad news was that it was time for the swim test. Some choice she had, Alicia thought—the Duchess of Bagglesnort or drowning!

As they headed back from the Salon de Beauté, which Kristen had already renamed the Snorty's Snotty Saloon, Alicia said, "I can't bear that woman!"

"Who, Snorty?" Kristen replied.

"*Acht*, Snorty!" Gundersnap giggled. "I like that!"

Alicia stopped on the landing and said, "I think the duchess is so mean."

"Me too," said Kristen. "I don't care if I am a flame child, or whatever she called me."

Alicia looked at her turretmates. "You both look vonderful!" she cried gleefully.

"Vonderful! Vonderful!" the three princesses yelled as they ran down the steps and across a small balcony to the winding staircase that led to their rooms.

Chapter 10

TESTING ONE, TWO, THREE—GLUB!

Inside the main salon of the South Turret, they found Lady Merry in a state of excitement.

"My water wings!" exclaimed Lady Merry as Gilly and the other maids entered with baskets of beach towels, bathing garments, and bathing tiaras.

"You shall all be taking your swim tests now. These are your bathing tunics," Gilly said to the princesses. Each of the maids held up an official Camp Princess bathing costume. They were the oddest-looking garments the three princesses had ever seen. Made from cloth of gold, they were neither gown nor trousers.

"Why in the name of Neptune do we have to wear bathing tiaras?" Kristen asked.

"Camp rule," Gilly replied crisply. "Rule eighteen, section six, article two, under Sports and Athletics, says, 'All princesses must wear the regulation bathing tiaras. These are conveniently attached to a cap to protect the hair and they do have some flotation built in as well.'"

Then Gilly added, "One must always appear royal, wet or dry. No exceptions—except with Frankie, the riding counselor. You'll meet her next session. She's out on a pony trek with some of the Third Years."

"Swimming should be an exception too. How are we supposed to swim with this contraption on our heads?" Kristen was absolutely fuming.

"Now, now, Kristen." Lady Merry was shaking a finger at Kristen, who was truly a bright-red flame child at the moment. "Let's not make a royal stink out of this. Just be the royal good sport that I know you are and show us your mettle, dear. I hear that you are perfection itself in the water—fast and powerful."

"You can bet your water wings on that, Lady Merry!" Kristen said as she slammed the bathing tiara on her head and began to strip down right in the salon to put on her tunic. The maids turned white. Lady Merry rose out of her reinforced rocker in a near fit. Alicia and Gundersnap feared she might be having a stroke or heart attack!

"Kristen, Kristen! Not here in our salon. Please, child, into your chamber to change!"

"Oh, all right." Kristen stomped off to her chamber with her dress half on and half off.

"Come! Come quickly, Princesses," Lady Merry said when the three girls emerged from their chambers dressed for their swim tests. "We must be off."

To "be off" was never a simple matter with a person of the amplitude of Lady Merry. A whiskered gentleman arrived with several young assistants. With their help, the generously proportioned lady climbed into an ornate sedan chair with curtains and a fringed canopy on top to provide shade.

"Now I'm just going to slip into something more comfortable," Lady Merry said as she lowered the curtains. Soon the sedan chair began to toss and buck like a ship caught in a sudden gale.

"She's changing into her bathing costume," said an attendant as a large corset was flung through the curtains. Finally Lady Merry pulled back the curtain. She was sitting in the sedan chair in a brilliant crimson-and-purple polka-dot silk costume. "I wear both teams' colors, please note."

The three princesses did note the colors as well as the size of the costume.

"Ah, yes, it took two jousting tents to make this outfit. Ever so clever, isn't it?" Lady Merry said.

The princesses, along with several others and Lady Merry still in the sedan chair, made their way across the drawbridge. They headed down the grassy banks that surrounded the moat to a small crescent of beach, where Lady Gustavia, one of the waterfront counselors, sat in a tall stone chair. She wore a golden ruby-studded whistle around her neck to catch the attention of those swimmers who were not obeying the strict waterfront safety rules.

The moat was fairly wide and encircled the entire castle. Some of the older princesses said it was really fun to swim under the drawbridge.

"No dangerous fish?" Alicia asked a third-year princess named Eloise.

"Oh, no, just lovely little sunfish mostly. They are quite friendly. They come up and tickle your toes."

"How deep is it?" asked Gundersnap nervously.

"It's over your head out in the middle. The shallow parts go pretty far out, so don't worry."

"But the best part about the moat," Princess Eloise continued, "is that it gives you great views of the castle. When you learn how to float on your back, there is nothing nicer than just floating along and looking up at all the lovely turrets and spires. You can smell all the good food cooking as you go by the kitchens and hear the blacksmith in his yard hammering away. On the far side of the moat, the one you can't see from here, the banks are covered with daffodils in the spring. And look, the water is so blue. Just like your sapphires, Kristen. It reminds me of a sapphire ring." Princess Eloise was known for being a very kind princess, and all the younger girls wanted to be just like her.

"Brrr, it's cold," Alicia said as she stuck a dainty toe in.

"Not really," said Kristen. "Not nearly as cold as in the Isles of the Salt Tears. What about in Sloboland, Gunny?"

"I don't go swimming at home," Gundersnap explained. "Mummy is afraid we might die before we get married. She has all our husbands picked out already, and she has to pay big money if we die."

Alicia was suddenly grateful that her own Belgravian royal family didn't believe in arranged marriages. She hoped Gundersnap's chosen husband would be a nice one.

The three princesses now turned to watch the attendants in the launching of Lady von Schleppenspiel. Lady Merry created a rather large disturbance in the calm surface of the moat's waters as she paddled out to the center. She then twirled about in her water wings and began waving at the princesses of the South Turret. "Good luck on your swim tests, Princesses!" She blew them kisses as she bobbled about in the clear water.

The swim test would begin from the small sandy beach on which they now stood. Those who were already swimmers, such as Kristen and Myrella, were in the water about to begin their circuit of the moat. They were supposed to circle the castle clockwise, then swim under the drawbridge and back to the starting point.

It seemed like no time since Kristen and Myrella had started, but suddenly they heard "A-ten level!" Lady Gussie shouted this as Kristen and Myrella raced under the drawbridge in the last stretch toward the beach.

"Tie!" Myrella called out.

A tie it was indeed. Myrella had almost beaten Kristen, but Kristen had pulled even at the very last second.

"Let's do it again," Kristen said.

"No, I want to do tricks," Myrella replied as she clambered up on a rock in the middle of the moat. She dived off in a stunning upside-down twist. Ringlets of hair sprang out from her bathing tiara in a bright golden flurry.

"One might think she had scales," said a nasty voice behind them. Alicia turned to look. It was the Duchess of

Bagglesnort. She smiled her rather grim smile and said, "But then again, what would one expect from a princess of the Marsh Kingdoms?"

Alicia and Gundersnap exchanged looks.

"Omigod, does she suck or what?" Kristen muttered.

Alicia shivered in the sun at the test of bravery confronting her—the swim test. "If Kristen and Myrella are A-tens," Alicia whispered to Gundersnap, "We're probably Z-subzeros."

"I don't see why we have to take a test. We told them we can't swim. What's there to test? How bad we are?" said the ever-practical Gundersnap.

But the time was coming. The two princesses stood on the small beach with a dozen other princesses waiting their turns.

And then Alicia and Gundersnap were called.

"By the frosty breath of Saint Bertie, it's really cold," Alicia gasped as she waded in cautiously. Then she sent up a quick prayer to Saint Addie of Vernon, the patron saint of swimmers.

"Not so cold when you have as much padding as I do," Lady Merry said. "Come, come, miladies. Follow me. The water wings will support you."

"Lead them once around the moat, Lady Merry. We just want to see their form with the wings," Lady Gussie called.

Her teeth chattering, Alicia felt her feet leave the sand as the bottom of the moat slanted downward toward the middle, where the water would be over their heads. The water wings held her up! It was not quite as scary as she had imagined.

"Now, stroke toward me, girls," Lady Merry instructed.

Lady Merry cut a large wake through the water. The waves she made lapped gently over the two princesses, but they managed to keep up. They circled around the castle, by the blacksmith's shop where they heard the hammer and tongs as he fitted the shoes to horses, by the kitchen where the wonderful fragrance of plum tarts baking wafted out across the moat.

As they swam, Alicia looked up and wondered where in this castle might an unfinished tapestry be. Aside from the turrets for the princesses, there were many more towers and spires than she would have ever guessed. They continued swimming and were soon passing under the drawbridge. It was all shadows and strange echoes.

"Woo, woo!" Lady Merry called out, and the hollow sounds of the echoing drawbridge wrapped around the two princesses. "I'm a ghost!" Lady Merry giggled as if she were one of the campers. "I'm a ghost!"

"Holy monk bones, is she trying to scare us?" Alicia

paddled faster as she approached the beach where they had started. Lady Gussie waded out to greet them.

"Bravo, Your Highnesses," said Lady Gussie. "Now for the final test."

"What's that?" Alicia asked.

"Faces in the water," Gussie replied.

"No!" both princesses gasped.

"Oh, yes!" Princess Myrella said. She was jumping up and down on the beach. "It's fun. Just close your mouth and open your eyes. You'll see the loveliest little fish."

Princess Alicia had no desire to see lovely little fish. She had no desire to get her face wet. All she could think of was getting water up her nose. The whole idea was appalling. Who would dare to go first? She turned to Gundersnap, who was looking quite pale.

"*Acht!* This is . . . scary!"

Alicia was relieved to see that Gundersnap was scared too, but before she knew it, Gundersnap had plunged her head under the water. When she resurfaced, she was indeed spouting water from her nose, and her bathing tiara was perched at an odd angle.

Gundersnap blinked, then sputtered. "I opened my eyes. I saw a fish that looked exactly like my mother! Totally ice!"

"Oh, it must have been the prickly blowfish," Lady Gussie offered.

"*Ja, ja.* It was blown up like a balloon and had little stickers all over its scales."

"Very good, Princess Gundersnap," said Lady Gussie. "Well, now we can put you in the advanced beginners class. Anyone who can put her head under can be a B-eight. Two more levels and you'll be an intermediate, out of the moat, and ready for the lake."

Alicia stared at Gundersnap in amazement. How had she done it? B-8! If she didn't do it, Alicia supposed she would be a B-flat! Left behind on the beach of the moat while her turretmates went off for lake swimming.

The princess squished her eyes shut—she had no intention of seeing the blowfish that looked like the Empress Maria Theresa of All the Slobodks. She held her nose and stuck her head into the water. She was tempted to open one eye. But no. All they said was to get your face wet, not your eyeballs. She could still be a B-8 with her eyes shut. Her cheeks blew out. Air . . . I need air . . . is this long enough? Alicia thought as she burst through the water's surface. She was sputtering and gasping, but she felt quite pleased with herself. Aunt Molly never did this! she thought. So ice!

"Hooray! Hooray!" Myrella, Gundersnap, and Kristen

were now clapping. Princess Alicia smiled. How curious, she thought. She had heard cheering crowds before. Whenever she and Mum and Pop and her sisters marched in a parade, the citizens of Belgravia would applaud them. But this was somehow different. She was now being cheered not simply for being a princess, but for being a wet princess—a princess who had accomplished something! How curious indeed. She felt a strange, wonderful new feeling of confidence.

"Congratulations, Alicia." Kristen came up and gave her a hearty slap on the back that jostled Alicia's bathing tiara more than the dunking had.

There was a sudden cool breeze, and everyone's teeth began to chatter.

"Oh, my stars and Saint Delphine's corset, I swear it's autumn coming on again!" cried Lady Merry. "Come, Princesses, out of the water before you catch your death of cold."

Lady Gussie was tweeting her whistle and waving her arms from the stone lifeguard chair. "Everyone out of the water!"

"Who's Saint Delphine, Lady Merry?" Gundersnap asked as a bathing maid was drying her off.

"My patron saint, the saint of ample ladies. She was

about the size of that turret over there." Lady Merry pointed toward one of the smaller turrets.

"No!" all three princesses said at once.

The princesses returned to the South Turret. When Alicia entered her chamber, Gilly was setting out her clothes. "I think you'll need your fur-lined underclothes. It's getting cold, and it's been a long day for you," she said as she bustled around the room. "Let's see, how many seasons since morning—at least two, because it wasn't summer when you were with Duchess of Bagglesnort, then it was summer, and now it certainly looks like winter will be setting in. And you've been swimming. Oh, it tires me out just to think about it."

"How can that be, Gilly? You must be much more tired. You dressed yourself, and then you dressed us and brought our food."

"Oh, I'm used to it, milady," Gilly replied with a smile. She then paused in her bustling and looked at Alicia. She had known a lot of princesses, but there was something special about Alicia. She seemed exceptionally sweet and kind, and not at all snooty. She didn't take her royalty for granted as so many other princesses did.

"I think it will be coziest, Your Highness," Gilly said, "if you take your supper in the turret this evening. Everyone is quite exhausted. No sense having to get dressed for dinner."

"That is a good idea, Gilly. Can we wear our night-gowns, night cloaks, and cut slippers?" Alicia asked.

"Absolutely. Listen to the howl of that wind straight over the plains of Wesselwick. That's always the coldest wind."

After their supper, and after Lady Merry had excused herself, the girls played Parcheesi in front of the fire as they sipped cocoa.

"In Slobodkonia," Gundersnap was saying, "we play this game using servants for pieces."

"What?" exclaimed Kristen.

"Yes, Empress Mummy had a huge Parcheesi board made from big tiles in the central courtyard of the castle. We have the servants dress as pieces and then direct them where to go."

"How appalling," Alicia said.

Gundersnap blinked. "You think so?"

"I most certainly do. Servants should be servants. They are people, not toys."

"You are very smart, Alicia." Gundersnap turned to Kristen. "And you are too. I am glad that I have you as tur-retmates."

"Me too," Kristen and Alicia both said at once.

"Let's make a pact," Kristen said. "Let's promise always to be mates in the South Turret through every session."

In the South Turret? Alicia wondered. But she did not hesitate. She thrust her hands into the center of the circle and held on to the others' until there were six hands clasped in what was known as the Royal Hand Pact. This meant they would always be friends and allies and always come to one another's aid wherever, whenever, and for whatever reason—in love, in war, in sickness, and in health.

When they withdrew their hands, Alicia looked slowly at her mates. "Princesses, I have a very serious question."

"Vot is it, Alicia?" Gundersnap leaned forward.

"Do you believe that there really is a ghost in the South Turret?"

"I don't believe in ghosts," Gundersnap said. "I can't see them, so they don't exist."

"Look, if there *are* ghosts, what's to be afraid of? It's not like a great white shark," Kristen said, touching the shark's tooth that she wore as a pendant around her neck.

"How can you wear that around your neck while you sleep, Kristen?" Gundersnap asked.

"Because I know it's dead, like a ghost. My harpoon killed it."

But hello! You can't kill a ghost, Alicia thought. That's the whole point. It's dead, and it comes back to haunt you for some reason.

They had only been at Camp Princess for four days, but on two of those nights Alicia had sensed upon awakening that there might have been a presence in her bedchamber while she slept. Tomorrow would be the fifth day of camp. That left nine more days for this first session. Would she feel this spirit each night? she wondered.

Another thought struck her. Nine more days meant she didn't have much time to teach her songbird how to sing! That thought was almost as alarming as notions of ghosts. She would have to go to Princess Roseanna, the Mistress of the Aviary and Songbird Counselor, to seek her advice.

Alicia noticed that her songbird seemed the slightest bit happy only when she was reading *Love Letters of a Forgotten Princess*. If she happened to look up as she read, she could see an almost wistful look in the golden bird's eyes. Sometimes she thought he might even be on the brink of singing. If only that would happen, Alicia thought, she'd be the happiest camper at Camp Princess.

Chapter 11

THE PRINCESS PARLOR

The next morning there was a cold drizzle falling outside the castle, which meant there would be no swimming or archery or falconry. After needlepoint the three princesses decided to go to the Princess Parlor, where the campers often gathered on rainy days to play checkers, practice with their songbirds, drink cocoa, and toast marshmallows.

"Maybe the smell of cocoa will loosen up your bird's vocal cords," Kristen said hopefully as they entered the pink and silver parlor. Alicia was carrying her weeb in its cage. She set the cage on a stand and stood hopelessly as she listened to another bird sing an aria, a song from an opera.

"Still no luck, Princess Alicia?" Princess Eloise looked up from the chess game she was playing with Princess Myrella. Princess Eloise was as pretty as she was kind. Her auburn hair fell in cascades of ringlets to her shoulders. Her eyes were a rich, deep brown, and dimples flashed in her cheeks when she smiled.

"No luck," replied Alicia. "And I had a consultation with Princess Roseanna. But nothing seems to work." What I need is a wizard like Merlin, she thought, not for the first time. Merlin's magic would make the weeb sing.

"You know, Alicia, my very first session here my song-bird sang, but it had a hideous voice. I think I might have preferred if she hadn't sung," Eloise said with a smile.

How did Princess Eloise always seem to know exactly the right thing to say? Alicia was so glad that she was on the Purple team too.

"Come over to the piano. Let me play some scales for the bird," said Gundersnap. But even with music, the bird did not sing. Alicia looked at her weeb sadly. She felt like she was going to cry.

When Gundersnap saw this, she stopped playing and jumped up. "*Vrachtun!*" The word fired from her mouth like a bullet from a musket. Her eyes narrowed as she looked at

Alicia's bird. "Enough of this, you lazy veeb. Sing! I command you to sing for your mistress!"

The bird blinked, turned in its cage, and dropped a splat of white.

"That does it." Gundersnap opened the cage door and reached in.

"What are you doing, Gundersnap?" Princess Eloise cried out.

"Don't vorry." Gundersnap held the bird upside down and began to shake it like a saltshaker. "Sing! Sing!"

Other princesses dropped their marshmallow sticks in the fire and gathered around in dismay.

"Stop it!" Alicia cried. "You'll kill him."

"Nonsense," snapped Gundersnap. "My mother always shook us like this when we were little and misbehaving. It shakes out the nonsense. *Nicht nocklepop*, eh, bird?"

"Please stop, Gundersnap. I can't bear it," Alicia cried.

Gundersnap stopped, surprised. She shrugged, then turned the bird right side up and returned it to the cage. "I only vanted to help," she said softly.

Princess Eloise looked at Alicia with great sympathy and said, "This happens sometimes, especially with male weebs."

"But I feel so bad, Princess Eloise. I know that this contest counts for a lot. The Purple team needs all the good songbirds it can get. I know it's been a long time since we've won the Color Wars."

"That it has been!" said a princess named Lana, who was a Crimson.

But Princess Kinna said, "You know, I've heard that if you go out on a snowy and moonlit night and find a female weeb, that will make a male weeb sing."

"Really?" Alicia asked. Could she do that? At night? Would that really make him sing? She couldn't bear to be the princess who was responsible for losing the most important contest of the Color Wars.

"There are no shortcuts with a weeb," Princess Eloise said. "Just patience. Princess Kinna, those are just old tales."

Princess Kinna shrugged and went to sit by the fire.

It's so embarrassing, Alicia thought, being the only princess with a nonfunctioning songbird! And to think Gundersnap's bird not only knows how to sing but to march as well. Born to rule, that girl!

A few Crimson princesses who were sitting by the fireplace began to giggle and steal glances at Alicia as she stood with her stubborn bird. Kinna exploded out of the armchair. The one hundred and forty-eight braids that were laced with strings of diamonds trembled as she spoke a rather fierce-sounding language to the snickering girls. Even though the princesses did not understand what she was saying, they looked taken aback by her outburst.

"All right," Kinna said calmly, "I see my words need no translation. As captain of the Purples, I remind you that I have the right to report you for poor sportsmanship and unprincesslike behavior in the face of competition. This would result in demerits for your total team score." Her black eyes glistened like river stones.

There were no more snickers about Alicia and her bird.

Chapter 12

A RUSTLING IN THE NIGHT

More than a week had passed since Alicia caught her bird, and still it remained fiercely silent. There were only a few days left before the songbird contest. The motto that the Queen Mum had proclaimed kept ringing in Alicia's ears: "If one can teach a songbird to sing beautifully, one can lead a nation. Remember, Princesses, you were born to rule." Alicia pictured herself on the island she was supposed to rule—not on a throne, but in an ice-cream wagon, selling snow cones, or worse! If only the stubborn weeb would cooperate and sing.

She heard a knock on her chamber door. "Come in," she called.

It was Kristen.

"I've come to help. Look at this." She held up a funny little whistle. "It's a pitch pipe."

"What does it do?" Alicia asked.

"Maybe it will help your bird find his right tone. You know, his key. We can play the do-re-mi thing," Kristen said.

"Oh, I'm so sick of the whole do-re-mi thing," Alicia said with a sigh.

Just then Gundersnap and Myrella came in.

Gundersnap carried a small vial.

"What do you have there, Gunny?" Kristen asked.

"Honey! There is a saying you can catch more bees with honey than with vinegar."

"But he's not a bee, Gundersnap. He's a bird," Alicia said mournfully.

"This is a desperate situation, is what it is. Come on, let's try it," Kristen said.

"Come on, do try," Myrella urged.

"Has being sweet worked for you, Myrella, with those awful turretmates?" Alicia asked.

"Not really, but then again, they were born sour."

Gundersnap walked over and put two drops in the weeb's cup with an eyedropper.

"This doesn't sound like a remedy your mother the empress tried with you, Gundersnap," Alicia said.

"*Nachtung*, never. No. She dosed us with vinegar once a month. She said it made us strong."

Alicia and Kristen exchanged looks. It was their fervent hope that they would never have to meet Maria Theresa, Empress of All the Slobodks.

The princesses waited. The honey did nothing. The bird remained silent.

Luckily there were other activities besides songbird training in the days to come. Alicia loved jewelry design and making lanyards with semiprecious stones. And in upcoming sessions, there were going to be campfires and sleep-outs by the lake, the Purple team in their purple silk tents, the Crimson team in crimson silk tents. There would be more canoeing, which Alicia was becoming quite good at, and sailing. Alicia was also very skilled at falconry, which was the sport of hunting with birds. Teaching songbirds to sing was more difficult than teaching falcons to do double air flips!

Alicia, Kristen, and Gundersnap had just returned to their chambers from the archery field. Gundersnap was stomping around, singing a popular Slobodkonian marching tune. Her bird was chirping along quite nicely. Kristen had managed to teach hers a sea shanty. And Alicia once again tried to get her stubborn little weeb to sing the scales. Still nothing.

"I don't think that I have a bit of talent for this, Lady Merry. It took me forever even to catch this bird. I have a learning disability. I am songbird challenged."

"Nonsense, Your Highness," replied Lady Merry. "I shan't hear of it. The only thing you lack is patience. Give it time."

After dinner there was a knock on the turret door.

"Yes," trilled Lady Merry. "State your business. The hour is late."

"A package has arrived for Princess Alicia."

"Oh, my package!" Alicia exclaimed. "At last!"

A few minutes later, Alicia opened her box in the privacy of her bedchamber. There was a note from her father.

> *Dearest Alicia,*
> *I hope you are finding camp fun as well as a challenging experience. I know that you are up to any challenge. For you are my brave Alicia, and in your heart you are no puffball princess.*
> *Love and Kisses,*
> *Pop*

I hope I'm brave, she thought. "Oh, I miss them so much!" Alicia whispered, picking up the silver-fox muff and rubbing it against her cheek. She even put on the earmuffs, though it was summer outside. Then she got up and peered into the cage at the difficult bird. "Perhaps tomorrow you shall sing?" But the bird only looked back as if to say, "Perhaps not!" Alicia sighed.

Well, she thought, she might as well not waste time worrying. She turned to *Love Letters of a Forgotten Princess*. As she picked up the book, she looked at the bird. She had been right. His gaze did soften whenever she opened the book. Cautiously she stepped toward the cage, still holding the book open but pressed to her chest. There was a sudden mad fluttering as the bird hurled itself against the wire. Alicia gave a little shriek. A golden feather floated down toward the floor. She stooped to pick it up, and when she rose up again the little bird cocked his head and looked at her. There was intelligence in his eyes that made Alicia feel he was trying to tell her something.

Suddenly Alicia understood. "I must let you out, mustn't I?" she whispered. Somehow she knew that the bird would not fly away. When she opened the door of the cage, the bird flew directly to her bedpost and perched there, seeming to wait for Alicia to begin reading.

She had left the cage door open so he could return whenever he wanted. But he stayed where he was. He seemed in fact to be reading over her shoulder. When she grew very sleepy, she tucked the golden feather between the pages to mark her place. As she drifted off, she felt something rustle in one corner of her chamber. Did the room grow cold? Did she hear the songbird finally trill in the night? Was it words she had heard, the muffled voices of a man and a woman? Or were words from the book lacing through her dreams?

"For heaven's sake, Your Highness, what's your bird doing out of the cage?" Gilly said as she entered the chamber with Alicia's breakfast tray.

"Oh, my goodness." Alicia yawned sleepily. "He's still there." She rolled over and looked up at the bedpost, where the weeb was perched. He gave her an interested but not unfriendly look. All this time she had been waiting for him to sing. But now Alicia had the strangest feeling that the weeb was actually waiting for her to do something.

"What?" she said aloud. The bird opened his beak this time, very wide, but no sound came out.

"Are you talking to me, milady?" Gilly turned from ironing the tea gowns.

"Oh, no, Gilly. No, just . . . nothing."

Gilly gave Alicia a close look. "Well, the weather looks good, milady. It will be falconry this morning, then canoeing."

"Oh, how nice."

"You'll be using your special falconry glove, I take it. Quite the envy of the other campers."

"I'd like to wear my purple suede britches with the violet waistcoat for falconry. And then what for canoeing? It's a race, and no tiaras are required during races," said Alicia.

"Oh, a race!" Gilly said. "If only the Purples can win! You are a bit behind the Crimsons."

"Don't remind me," Alicia said glumly.

"Ah, but the Purples have been known to come from behind, milady. Strong finishers they can be!"

"Let's hope so. Can you help me figure out what to wear?"

"Princess Kristen always wears those lightweight silk pantaloons with the matching vest and the plumed hat."

"Yes, I know, but I think the pantaloons make my butt look big."

"Oh, nonsense, milady!"

"Are there going to be any princes on the river from Camp Burning Shield?" Alicia asked.

"No, no. They're having their boar hunt this week."

"Don't tell Princess Kristen. She'll run off to join them—and not for the princes but the boars. She loves hunting."

"Ah, she's a tomprincess all right, that one," Gilly replied.

Certainly not a puffball, thought Alicia. "I'd better wear the pantaloons; they're easier to paddle in," she said to Gilly. "And with only three days until the songbird contest, we Purples need every point we can get!"

Chapter 13

THOSE CHEATING CRIMSONS!

"One, two, *power stroke*! One, two, *power stroke*!" Princess Kinna, in the bow of the canoe, set the pace. Princess Alicia was in the stern. Kinna was a powerful paddler. Alicia had to match her stroke for stroke. If her bird couldn't sing, she could at least help the Purples by paddling.

In the lead was a Crimson canoe with Princess Morwenna and Princess Zelenka. Perhaps Kristen and Maggie of Schottlandia would catch them, or perhaps she and Kinna would, Alicia thought with great excitement.

They were coming into the final bend of the river. Kinna, an experienced river paddler, had told Alicia that heading for the outside of the curve would give them a boost from the current. But Kinna was not the only paddler who knew this. All three canoes were now heading for the outside of the bend.

Maggie and Kristen pulled ahead of the Crimsons' canoe. Good! thought Alicia. She saw Zelenka look around and say something to Morwenna. Then suddenly Kristen's canoe seemed to go off course. "Foul!" Maggie called.

"I don't believe it!" Princess Kinna said. The Crimsons had slammed the Purples' canoe! "That's cheating!" But there was no one on the riverbank to see it.

Princess Morwenna looked back, then turned her face to heaven. Who's she praying to, Alicia wondered. The patron saint of cheaters? "Well, by Saint Timothy, the patron saint of canoeing," Alicia muttered, "we'll overtake her!"

Then Kinna shouted, "Ramming speed!"

Alicia had never paddled so hard. She remembered Kinna's advice: It's all in the shoulders. That's where the power comes from. Hers were aching. But it was paying off. They were sweeping alongside the Crimson canoe now.

Now the real race began! It was the last hundred feet, bow to bow. The princesses onshore were screaming their heads off. The Purple and Crimson cheerleaders had torn off their tiaras and were waving them madly in the air.

There were cries of "Go Purple!" "Go Crimson!" "Go Kinna!" "Go Zelenka!" Someone yelled out, "Pray and paddle, Morwenna!" Alicia heard, "You can do it, Alicia!" From the corner of her eye she saw Gunny, stomping on the bank, rallying the team.

"Tie!" Lady Gussie called out as both canoes glided across the finish line at the exact same moment.

"Tie!" Alicia flopped back in the canoe. "If only we could have stroked a little bit harder. We could have won!"

"They haven't seen the last of us," Kinna said grimly. "Come on, let's go."

"Go where?"

"To congratulate the Crimsons," Princess Kinna said as they pulled up onto the riverbank. She climbed out of the canoe and began to walk toward Zelenka and Morwenna. The tall princess had her one hundred and forty-eight braids pulled back into a large ponytail. Alicia followed her reluctantly, keeping her eyes fastened on the bobbing cluster of braids.

"Congratulations, sister princesses." Kinna made a shallow curtsey. Morwenna and Zelenka looked somewhat startled.

"That's what I like to see!" Lady Gussie boomed. "Royally good sportsmanship!"

Kinna stepped closer to the princesses.

"You know what we do to cheaters in Mattunga?" she whispered. Kinna was trembling so hard with barely concealed anger that her braids shivered.

"We dangle them over the crocodile pit. To cheat is an insult to your god, your family, and your ancestors. And you know what?"

"What?" Zelenka said weakly.

"They never cheat again."

"We didn't cheat, and there are no crocodiles here," Morwenna said smugly.

"I'm sure we can arrange something," Kinna said. Then she turned and walked away.

Chapter 14

CASTLED!

The following evening the three princesses of the South Turret slid into their places in the Great Hall with their hair still slightly damp from swimming. They had been practicing hard for the swimming meet. Gundersnap and Alicia had both learned how to swim very quickly and would be competing against the Crimsons in their B-1 level. Even having tied the canoe races, they were still behind the Crimsons.

It seemed as if everywhere one turned in the castle, there was either a banner or a hanging scroll announcing the score for the Color Wars. The end of the first session would arrive soon, and tensions were mounting. All the campers talked about were the upcoming competitions.

The Duchess of Bagglesnort was, unfortunately, at their table, and she did not approve of sports talk during meals. She gave the girls a sharp look. "I would expect wet hair from Her Royal Frogginess," she said, glancing at Princess Myrella, "but not from you three."

Why was she always picking on the tiny princess? Alicia thought. This has to stop. But do I really have the nerve, she wondered. Or am I just a puffball princess? Yes, I have the nerve. I am no puffball princess. I was born to rule! She stood and pulled herself up to her full height. Her full height was not all that tall, but still she looked regal and every inch a princess.

"Duchess of Bagglesnort, your cruel words, spoken to the gracious and honorable Princess Myrella of the Kingdom of the Marshes, were hurtful, perhaps by accident—yes, I am sure by accident. Please, Your Grace, tell the Princess Myrella that you did not mean to hurt her."

A tide of red color began to rise beneath the powder on the duchess's cheeks. A hideous transformation swept across her face. Her eyes became angry slits.

"Sit down, Princess," the duchess hissed at Alicia.

"I prefer to stand," Alicia said quietly.

"Suit yourself." The Snort's voice had a deadly edge. "I will tell you, Princess, that you have no idea what my intentions were, are, or shall be. But I will say this: The Duchess of Bagglesnort does not do anything accidentally. How dare you, a mere child, tell me what to do? I am your superior."

"You are my superior in age, but not in rank. May I remind you that a princess always outranks a duchess."

Hatred oozed from the slits of the duchess's eyes. "You are castled!"

"Castled?" Alicia said with disbelief.

"Indeed, for the remainder of this session."

The members of the Purple team gasped. Short of being sent back to one's kingdom, being castled was the worst and most humiliating punishment there was at Camp Princess. It meant that a princess could not leave the stone confines of the castle, so all outdoor activities were forbidden. And when she was not at an activity, she had to remain in her turret. This was a real blow to the team. Alicia's bird might not be singing, but she had proved herself a strong paddler and was a crack falconer. The Purples needed her.

Chapter 15

BIRD, BOOK, AND SPIRIT

"I shall protest, my dear! I believe it is sheer nonsense that you should be castled."

"But that's not the only thing, Lady Merry," Alicia said. "Poor Myrella. It's not only the Snort—I mean, the Duchess of Bagglesnort—who picks on her. It's her turret-mates as well."

"Which turret is she in?"

"North."

"Oh, yes, a difficult group of princesses. But you know, my dear, changing turrets is nearly impossible during a session. Perhaps we can hope for next session, but not this one.

But now quick, child, bring me my lap desk and writing tools. We're going straight to the Queen Mum. I know she will be most sympathetic." Lady Merry drew her hanky from the bodice of her dress and began wiping her brow.

"Gilly, call my corset maid to come and loosen my stays. I can't write all trussed up like a stuffed goose. Got to get blood to the old brain. Now, don't you worry, dearie. We'll have you back in action shortly."

At least I told Old Snorty a thing or two, Alicia thought as she returned to her bedchamber. Gilly had just finished helping her out of her many layers of clothes. Alicia had stood still as a statue as Gilly fussed with the numerous tie strings, hooks, and buttons, all the while muttering, "It simply isn't fair, Your Highness. Everyone knows that the old goat has to have it out for somebody every year. They say whipping boys went out of style years ago, but now, by Saint Sebastian's bones, I think that the Snort can be said to have herself a whipping princess."

Well, she won't have me! thought Alicia, flinging herself angrily on her bed. Then she happened to look at the weeb. She always left his cage door open now, so he was perched on her bedpost. It was hard to imagine she had ever been worried about a silly old songbird. Troubles changed minute by minute. Troubles that might seem huge a few minutes before were not worth a pinch of pigeon doo now! That thought made her giggle.

"What are you giggling about, milady?" Gilly asked. "It's not a giggling matter, I daresay."

"No, it's not, I suppose," Alicia said, wiggling into her lacy white nightgown. She shivered as she climbed into bed, and then turned and stared at the weeb again. He had perched on her bedpost to read over her shoulder. Then she suddenly remembered that the night before, she might have heard a trilling sound after she had fallen asleep.

She knew for sure now that she had felt a cold presence as she slept every night. It was almost like a mist, but a cold mist. It was a dream of snow and moonlight and, yes, bird-song!

Something was happening at night in her chamber. Whether it was a bird singing or a ghost visiting, she wanted to be awake, to hear it and to see it. Could it be a female weeb coming into the chamber while she slept? Could there be some connection between the bird and the presence and the book? Was the bird singing to the presence?

She decided to stay up—at least until the time when the night drank up the moon. She would read into the small hours of the morning. And then she might sleep. If the weeb sang, she wanted to hear it.

Alicia reached for her book and stroked its cover. She kept the weeb's golden feather as her bookmark. It was odd; sometimes she could have sworn she left it in one place, but when she opened the book the feather would be in another, as if calling her attention to a particular letter in the book. As Alicia began reading, she once more vowed to stay awake.

But then, as the moon rode high in the sky, she yawned, and her eyes began to feel heavy. She sat up straighter against the great mass of pillows. She needed to stay awake. She needed to find out if indeed there was a ghost, a spirit that was somehow linked to the bird. Why would it come back now, for a little mute songbird? She had to know. But eventually the words began to blur on the page, her head drooped, and her chin touched the lace flounce of her nightgown. She was asleep.

"Rats!" Alicia muttered as she sprang from her bed. How had she fallen asleep? It was still night, she noticed, as she pulled back the covers and got out of bed.

She went to her window. All the turrets and towers of the castle wore snowy peaked hats. "Winter again." She sighed. The drawbridge was up, but she could see that the moat had frozen over. There was a brilliance to the night. A glistening white blanket of snow covered the fields. The Forest of Chimes looked as if it were made of lace. The path of moonlight across the snow blazed silver and seemed to beckon her.

Alicia thought about Princess Kinna's remedy of finding a female weeb on a snowy night. I must go! I must! she decided. There was no choice in the Color Wars' songbird contest. She was castled and might not be able to participate, but this was about much more than a contest. This bird had to sing, and it was not just so the Purple team could win. No, this was not about Color Wars and winning. This was about something she could barely understand, something she sensed somewhere deep inside of her.

It didn't take Alicia long to gather what she would need. But like so many princesses, she had never really dressed herself. There were always maids to help with the many layers that a princess had to wear. It began with pantalettes, then went on to shifts and chemises and under-petticoats and over-petticoats and kirtles and gowns. Each had a different system of hooking, tying, lacing, or buttoning. It was impossible to do it alone. Most of these garments fastened up the back.

"Stupid clothes!" Alicia muttered. Her first decision was to turn them all around so she could see what she was doing. Who'd care if she wore the gown backward? No one would see her.

By the time she had pulled on her purple boots, she was sweating. She grabbed her snowshoes and a candle. Just before she was about to slip out of her chamber, she turned to the songbird and said, "I'll find you a mate, I promise." Then she turned, pulled up the hood of her cloak, and tip-toed out of her bedchamber and across the floor of the parlor, holding her snowshoes in one hand and a candle in the other.

Chapter 16

CHIMES IN A SNOWY NIGHT

From the South Turret, Alicia descended several flights of stairs. She passed a guard fast asleep at his post. She was walking quickly through the Portrait Gallery when she started to look at the paintings of queens and empresses who had attended Camp Princess.

The guard might be asleep, but not her mum! She could have sworn the eyes in the portrait of Flora Mathilda Elinora, once a princess and now Queen of All the Belgravias, were following her.

By the time she reached the Great Hall, her candle was flickering. There was only a minute left in the wick, maybe less.

Alicia raced across the Great Hall and pulled open the wooden door to the courtyard. As she stepped out into the cold air, the gleaming carpet of snow seemed to dare her to cross. She couldn't leave footprints. She would have to edge around the courtyard to the blacksmith's shop at a far corner. There was a gate that could be opened from the inside. This led to a passageway to the banks of the moat. During her swim classes, she had passed right by the door of this passageway. She could see it when she was swimming.

Cautiously she began her journey around the square of snow in the courtyard. Finally she reached the blacksmith's shop. She went through the gate and then began to thread her way down the winding passageway to the moat. Once there she strapped on her snowshoes. In the blink of an eye, she was across the frozen moat and moving over the snowy field.

The new snowshoes were fast. Soon she was hearing the sound of the chimes. Now, where to begin? Alicia wondered. Where would a small songbird be on a cold, snowy night?

She entered the forest. She wondered if she should just wait and let the birds come to her. If she held herself very still against the tree where she now stood, maybe they would think she was just another part of the tree, just an odd branch to perch on. A very odd one with earmuffs!

The shadows of the branches cast a dark, lacy design on the moon-bright snow. A bell from above fell with a muffled thud into the whiteness at her feet. Alicia saw that the hood of the bell was as thin and delicate as a leaf, yet it had not shattered. What a strange and magical place this was!

As she continued to stand by the tree, Alicia's vision grew sharper. She could make out the tiniest knotholes in a small tree a few feet away. Might a female weeb be roosting in one of these holes that was no wider than an egg? She peered at the tree. There were two knotholes side by side that looked almost like eyes—rather baggy eyes, at that. Then she noticed a kind of knob between the eyes that could have been a nose.

The bark of the tree moved! Alicia caught her breath as a figure stepped forward. Her heart skipped a beat or two. What in the world?

"Not in the world, my dear. In the Forest of Chimes. That is all. All one needs, some might say."

Standing before her was a woman, a very old woman, garbed in a tunic of bark and leaves. She was wearing a cloak made of moss, and her long, white hair was caught up in a net of spiderwebs. A spider or two hung about her ears. On her shoulder perched a peregrine, a large bird with a black hood of feathers. Would this crone help her find a female weeb?

"There is much to be done, girl, beyond finding you a songbird."

On the bones of Saint George's dragon, how does this crone— Alicia's thoughts were interrupted by the words of the old woman.

"Now, now, girl, don't be swearing on poor old Saint George's beast and don't be calling me a crone. So, you wonder how I know what you are thinking? It's my gift, girl, my gift. With some it's harder to read the mind than others. But you're clear, girl. Clear as the clapper in the tree bells that chime. You're true. That is why you were chosen."

"Chosen? Chosen for what?"

The ancient woman stepped forward. She smelled like pine trees. She was very short—she only came up to Alicia's chin. Her eyes were colorless but had a bright spot in them. Alicia quickly realized that it was a reflection of the moon.

"'Tis your fate, your destiny."

"Destiny?" Alicia was completely baffled. "Who are you?"

There was a *kack kack* sound.

"Hush, Percy," said the old woman. She reached up and stroked the peregrine's feathers. "I am Berwynna of the Chimes."

"Berwynna?" Alicia said.

"Think, girl, think hard," Berwynna said.

Alicia opened her eyes wide. Could this be like . . . like . . . Merlin? She had barely even finished the thought when Berwynna shrieked, "Like Merlin! I am the sister of Merlin! But I am nothing like him." The spiders quivering over her ears hoisted themselves up on their silken threads into the hair that was piled like a bird's nest on Berwynna's head.

"Merlin's sister? I didn't know he had one," Alicia said.

"Nobody does. It's always Merlin this, Merlin that!" Her voice was shrill. "It's enough to drive one mad."

Alicia collected herself. Merlin's sister? Had she not wished for just this very thing? A Merlin!

"What is my destiny?" Alicia asked again.

"You think I'm going to tell you right off the bat?" Berwynna asked.

As if on cue, a bat flew out from Berwynna's hair. "Yikes!" screeched Alicia, but she pressed on with her questions. "You claim there is much to be done. So what is it that I must do?"

"Look, my dear, you have proven your courage and your determination by coming into the forest on a cold night when you have been castled."

So she agrees that it was perhaps wrong that I was

castled, Alicia thought.

"Of course I agree. What do you take me for, a nitwit?" This time a very tiny insect crept out of her ear.

Holy monk bones, she's got lice! "Oh, yuck!" Alicia muttered.

"I'm a friend to all creatures. If some decide to live on me, far be it from me to evict them."

"But what is it that you want me to do?"

"Restless spirits lurk, my dear." Berwynna stepped closer to Alicia and stood on her tiptoes. The reflections of stars now danced in her eyes. Berwynna smiled and then began to speak in a singsongy voice that scratched the night.

> *"Now listen closely to my tale*
> *Though it may turn your pink cheeks pale.*
>
> *There's still a story incomplete;*
> *Look closely and you'll see, my sweet.*
>
> *Two spirits must be put to rest*
> *Until another dream is blessed,*
>
> *And then, when every stitch is sewn,*
> *Evil's work is o'erthrown."*

"What?" Alicia was completely confused.

Berwynna sank down from her tiptoes and rocked back on her heels. She folded her arms across her narrow chest and looked at Alicia with a smug little grin.

"Go figure" was all she said.

Chapter 17

A GHOST PRINCESS

When Alicia returned to her bedchamber, the little weeb looked at her hopefully. "I'm sorry," Alicia said. "I didn't find a mate for you tonight." She sighed, and it seemed as if the bird sighed with her.

Alicia looked at the clock on her mantel. It was just before midnight. Not even an hour had passed, but it seemed as if she had been gone for at least three. How strange! Alicia took off her backward clothes, put on her thinking tiara, and slipped into bed. She pulled the covers up to her chin while she stole another look at the clock. Had it all been a dream?

She repeated the strange, tiny woman's verse until it sang in her head. "Two spirits must be put to rest . . . when every stitch is sewn" . . . what could it mean? She looked across to the little bird and felt sorry for him. But a fat lot of good it had done her to sneak out on this bitter-cold night. All she had accomplished was to find a nutty old lady who spoke in nonsense rhymes.

Alicia picked up *Love Letters of a Forgotten Princess*. She had read some of these love letters over a hundred times and could recite many by heart. As she paged through the book to find her favorites, a few words in one of the letters caught her eye, as if for the first time.

"What is this?" she whispered to herself. As she read, Alicia felt her cheeks turn pale.

"Hidden in a turret the tapestry is lost, but its magic can be found between the seconds of midnight's chimes."

Alicia's head seemed to spin with glittering fragments of stories—words, rhymes, verses that began to stitch themselves together with new meaning. Words came back to Alicia. The words of that strange creature made of bark, moss, and magic—Merlin's sister, Berwynna! "And then, when every stitch is sewn, evil's work is o'erthrown."

There was a sudden rattling at the shutters. A cold draft swept through the chamber.

The weeb began to carol! His silvery notes filled the room.

Alicia was out of bed in a flash. "You sang! You sang!"

"That was not a song. It was a cry for help," a voice whispered. The voice seemed to come from the grate in the fireplace, where the coals still glowed. As another gust of wind pushed open the shutter, a shiver went up Alicia's spine.

"Who's there?" Alicia called. A swirl of snow blew down from the chimney. She was shaking so hard that her teeth chattered, but she forced herself to ask again, "Who's there, I say? Who needs help? The weeb?"

There was a hiss and a small puff of smoke and ash from the fireplace. The swirl of snow had been sucked into the fire, striking the coals, which were now sputtering.

Alicia ran to get the bellows to breathe life into the flames. It would be a cold morning if the coals in the fire went dead. She had seen Gilly pump the bellows. It didn't look hard. She crouched down and began pumping. The coals started to glow orange again. She pumped harder. A tiny flame began to flicker.

Then the shutters swung wide open and immense gusts of snow swept into her bedchamber.

The fire in the grate leaped up to meet the gusts. For a few brief seconds, snow and flames seemed to join in an odd dance. And then it was over.

A figure stepped out of the fire. It was a beautiful lady! Her dress hung like dim amber flames. Wisps of shimmering hair escaped from an old-fashioned headpiece, the medieval kind that was called a coif. On top of the coif was a small crown, a coronet. Alicia knew that only ruling princesses wore coronets! The coronet seemed to be made of snowflakes.

Now, at last, the weeb burst into a song of pure joy, and the strange princess smiled.

Alicia took a step closer to the princess, who quivered like a candle flame in the breeze. "Who are you?" Alicia whispered. "Are you a ghost?"

The woman nodded.

"Are you my destiny?" Alicia asked, remembering Berwynna's words. "Are you the spirit that must be put to rest?"

"We must both be put to rest, me and my love, too," the ghost princess said.

"Him? Who? How?" Alicia was completely confused.

"How, my dear? The tapestry is how you shall do it. The stitches left undone must be stitched, and then a spell will be broken."

"But how will I know what to stitch?"

"You shall know," the ghost princess said. "Follow me." She tipped her head toward the door of Alicia's chamber.

Alicia felt as if she were walking behind a fine mist shaped like a lovely lady. She could see right through to the stone walls of the castle. The ghost princess's dress gave off a strange light that lit the darkened passageway. They needed no candles.

As Alicia and the ghost princess wound their way through the corridors to the Portrait Gallery, the castle's great clock began to sound the hour. It was midnight. "Between the seconds of midnight's chimes," Alicia thought with excitement. She dared not steal a glance at her mother's portrait. The queen might disapprove, but Alicia had to go. This ghost was somehow connected with the weeb. Alicia was sure of that. But how? The princess might be a ghost, but she was the ghost of a princess and not the ghost of a female weeb.

They stopped in front of a portrait of a young princess. "This is you!" Alicia exclaimed.

"Yes, I was here as a girl, and later I returned."

Alicia put her hand on the corner of the frame. The portrait swung out from the wall, revealing a door. The ghost princess opened the door and appeared to float up a winding staircase. Alicia followed step by step.

The staircase seemed to spiral upward forever. When they reached the top, they were directly under the cone-shaped roof of the turret.

"I never knew this turret existed," Alicia said.

"It is a long-forgotten one. It was used as a storeroom when I was the needlework counselor here."

Alicia stopped. "You were a needlework counselor?"

The ghost princess turned on the stairs and nodded.

"You are the princess with the broken heart who took refuge here." Again the ghost princess nodded. "And this is the unfinished tapestry that you are taking me to, isn't it?" For a third time, the ghost princess nodded. Then she spoke.

"I am the Forgotten Princess that you have been reading about all this time. You see, my dear, our destinies are joined. Not only did you read about me, but you really believed in me and felt my troubles as if they were your own."

Alicia put a hand to her cheek in astonishment. The book that her sisters often teased her about reading was part of her destiny. She followed the ghost through the doorway at the top of the stairs.

They were in a small room. In the dim glow of the ghost princess's dress, Alicia could just make out a tapestry on the wall. She walked toward it as if in a trance. The woven cloth did not look like it had aged, but she could hardly make out the design. As Alicia lifted her finger to touch it, shapes seemed to appear through the cloth. It was almost as if ghost actors were walking onto a stage. Alicia saw a regal woman who wore a coif fixed by a coronet, and over the coronet, hanging like mist, was a long veil.

Alicia turned slowly around toward the lovely ghost. "This is you," Alicia said. The princess nodded.

Alicia couldn't help but feel that the princess looked familiar to her, and not just from the portrait. Something about her hair and sparkling eyes did indeed remind her of someone. She just couldn't remember who.

"What happened? How was your heart broken?"

"You know my story," the ghost princess said. "My name is Kyranala, and I come from the Kingdom of Kerrwyn. After my mother died, an evil princess from another kingdom lured my father into marriage. My poor sister had to go live with them. A short time later, my stepmother poisoned my father, and my sister managed to run away. My stepmother became known as Queen Guthstab the Remorseless. She terrified everyone.

"There was a small order of knights who remained loyal to my father's memory. They protected me. One of these knights, Sir Roland, and I fell deeply in love. We were married, secretly. But Guthstab found out, and she hated my happiness. She had the Blood Guard capture Sir Roland. She ordered him put to death. I ran here to Camp Princess, where my sister and I had been so happy. They let me stay on as the needlepoint counselor."

Alicia had been looking closely at the tapestry during the princess's story. As she spoke, the cloth began to suggest a design, a design to be stitched that told a story with great meaning. Alicia turned to the Princess Kyranala. "Do you have a needle and thread?"

"Right there, my dear." She pointed to a section of the tapestry where a needle was tucked in next to several others, all with different colored threads. Alicia began to stitch. She blinked in surprise. In no time she had done a perfect row of split stitches, and her fingers began to move even more rapidly.

"Goodness!" Alicia exclaimed. "I just did the butterfly stitch—that's the hardest stitch of all! My older sister can't even do that one!"

She felt a kind of energy traveling through the thread to the very tips of her fingers as she stitched. "This is like magic."

"Not like magic, my dear. It is magic."

Princess Kyranala's face seemed to glow now almost like

a living person's. It had a tinge of pink, as if blood coursed through her veins.

Can it make the dead live again? Alicia wondered. Am I bringing her back to life, or am I putting a spirit to rest?

Alicia sensed new urgency for her task now. She turned back to the tapestry and continued to sew. As she stitched, the figures became clearer. She began to see a forest of trees with shining crystal bells instead of leaves. She saw a small figure crouched behind a tree trunk. Could it be Berwynna? On another panel she saw a scene with a cage at the princess's feet.

"You are kneeling here at the edge of the Forest of Chimes. There is a cage, and inside I can see the outlines of a bird. A bird to be freed, or a bird to be stitched? Is the cage door opened or closed? I cannot tell." Alicia felt her heart beat rapidly. "What is it?"

"I have a long story to be stitched, too much for one night. The sky grows light, and you must be back in your bedchamber," replied the ghost princess.

"Please, can't I stitch the bird? He looks so much like my weeb." Alicia knew then that what she had suspected was true. The weeb and the spirit of this princess were connected in some mysterious way. Bird, book, and spirit! she thought.

Princess Kyranala seemed almost to read her mind. "You must wait just a bit longer. Tomorrow night, after the songbird contest, all will be revealed."

"Why must I wait?"

"The tapestry cannot be completed alone. You will need your friends. But do not take them to the tapestry until after the songbird contest. It is almost as if destiny has put you three princesses together, is it not?"

With those words the ghost princess vanished. And Alicia herself was no longer standing in the turret in front of the unfinished tapestry, but in her own chamber, barefoot on the cold stone floor, next to her bed. She was not sure how long she had been standing there or how she had returned from the forgotten turret. And she wondered what had happened to Princess Kyranala.

As the first streaks of dawn light slipped in through the window, she felt something cold and wet beneath her feet. She was standing in a puddle of water. Could the puddle have come from the snowflake coronet? Alicia wondered what was real and what had been a dream.

She turned to look for the weeb. He was not on her bedpost where she had last seen him and he was not in his cage. The cage was empty! She gave a small cry of dismay. The shutters were still open. Had the golden bird flown away?

Why, after all this, had he fled? Was he looking for his mate in the Forest of Chimes? She had to find him! He was at the center of this whole mystery. The bird and the ghost princess—the Forgotten Princess—were linked. Their fate depended on each other and on Alicia and her friends.

Did she dare go to the Forest of Chimes again? Would Berwynna know where to find the weeb? One thing was for sure—she must ask Kristen and Gundersnap to help. She must tell them this strange story. She must take them to the tapestry, after the songbird contest, as the ghost princess had instructed.

Chapter 18

UNCASTLED!

Last night's winter had turned to spring by the time Gilly brought her breakfast. Alicia ate quickly.

In the salon Lady Merry greeted her, waving a note from Queen Mum.

"Good news, Alicia!"

"What? What?" Kristen and Gundersnap had arrived in time to hear the news.

"Is she uncastled?" Kristen asked.

"Indeed she is," Lady Merry replied.

Gundersnap and Kristen began cheering wildly.

"And there is more good news, my dears," Lady Merry

continued with a smile.

"What's that?" Alicia asked.

"Well, I gave the Queen Mum the proposal Princess Gundersnap wrote about our little Myrella and how poorly her turretmates were treating her. She has graciously agreed to let Myrella join you next session!"

And now a near riot broke out. The princesses were jumping and hugging and throwing pillows into the air.

"Princesses! Princesses! You're behaving like savages. Please!" Lady Merry begged. But it was no use. The princesses' spirits were simply too high.

Lady Merry von Schleppenspiel sank back into her reinforced rocking chair. "Gilly . . . Gilly, dear, would you come and loosen my stays. The princesses are hogging all the air. I need to ease my breathing."

Alicia, no longer castled, was now free to join in all outdoor activities. The first of that day was the Picnic Royale. Gold tablecloths were spread on the grass by the lake, and a croquet field had been set up with silver wickets for the amusement of the campers. During the game Alicia could not find a minute alone with her turretmates to tell them of her lost bird and the story of the ghost princess. And when croquet ended, kite flying began in the meadow.

After a few minutes, Alicia slipped up to Kristen. "Reel in your kite and follow me." Kristen was about to protest. "If anyone asks, tell them that my kite got away and you're helping me look for it." Then she went over to Gundersnap and told her the same thing.

Alicia led her friends from the meadow into the Forest of Chimes.

"What's this all about?" Kristen asked.

"My weeb is gone. It flew away last night. And there is more. Much more. Just follow me."

There was such mystery surrounding this walk in the forest that Gundersnap and Kristen were afraid even to question Alicia. Finally Alicia decided that they had gone far enough.

"All right. Now we must just stand here quietly for a few minutes," Alicia said. She hoped that Berwynna would help find the weeb, but she was not quite sure how she would explain Berwynna to her friends.

"What's to explain?" A crotchety voice scraped through the tinkle of the chimes. "Gads! What a whiner you are!"

Kristen and Gundersnap jumped back in shock.

"Berwynna!" Alicia said with relief.

"No! The Duchess of Malta! Who else wears spiderwebs, leaves, and a moss tutu?"

Kristen and Gundersnap stared in disbelief at the peculiar figure standing in front of them. She was plucking at a short, fluffy moss skirt that she had pulled over her bark tunic. "How do you like it? I think it becomes me. Now, what are you grousing about this time?"

"My bird, my bird." Alicia had meant to be brave, but she found herself in tears.

"Here, blow your nose." Berwynna handed her a wad of cobwebs.

"Eeeew!" Gundersnap and Kristen wrinkled up their noses at the sight of the cobwebs.

Alicia, for the sake of being polite, took the cobwebs and tried not to make a face as she pretended to blow her nose in the icky things. Then she remembered her royal training.

"Berwynna," she said, "I'm pleased to introduce my turret-mates, Princess Kristen of the Isles of the Salt Tears in the Realm of Rolm, and Princess Gundersnap from the mighty Empire of Slobodkonia."

"I know," Berwynna said. "Continue."

"My weeb flew away, and tonight is the songbird contest and it had just begun to sing last night and . . . and . . ." It was again hard for Alicia to talk.

"And, and, and," Berwynna said in a mocking voice.

"Are you going to help Alicia find it?" Gundersnap demanded.

Berwynna did not answer the question but stepped closer to Alicia. As she had before, she rose on to her tiptoes. She looked directly into the young princess's eyes with her own clear ones that now reflected not the stars but patches of clouds drifting over the treetops. Then as before the scratchy voice began its song, or was it perhaps a riddle, Alicia wondered.

> *"A golden knight with heart so broke,*
> *A ghostly princess with one great hope.*
>
> *You've sewn some stitches, yes, my dear,*
> *But while they have made some things clear*
>
> *Your needlework has just begun.*
> *A cage is empty, a song unsung,*
>
> *But the song is not the end in sight;*
> *For this you need to stitch a knight."*

Berwynna stepped back with a satisfied grin. The princesses waited.

"Is that it, no more?" Alicia asked desperately.

"That's all, my dears." And, still grinning, Berwynna began to dissolve into the mists of the forest.

Kristen turned to Alicia. "Princess Alicia of All the Belgravias, would you puleeeze explain!"

"*Ja*, explain," Gundersnap said.

"It's a long story." Alicia sighed.

"I bet it is!" Kristen exclaimed.

"I'm not sure where to begin."

"The beginning, naturally," Gundersnap said.

"Well, the beginning was on the day I caught the weeb and then—do you remember when I asked you if you believed in ghosts the first week of camp?"

Kristen and Gundersnap both nodded. "I said they weren't practical," Gundersnap said.

"And I said they were nothing to be afraid of," Kristen added.

"Well, guess what—there *is* a real one."

And so Alicia told the long story of Princess Kyranala, the weeb, and the strange little crone named Berwynna who had told her of her destiny.

As she was concluding the story, she said, "But there is one more thing. The ghost princess told me that it was not merely my destiny to finish the tapestry. You both are a part of this as well. She told me it was almost as if destiny had made us turretmates."

The three princesses looked at one another. And they knew that the ghost princess was right. They shared more than a turret. They shared a destiny.

Chapter 19

THE SONGBIRD CONTEST

"So, dear princesses, the time has finally come." The Queen Mum paused dramatically. "We are gathered for the most important event of the Color Wars for this session: the songbird contest."

A roar of applause and shouts broke out from the princesses. Then the chanting started. "Go Crimson!" "Go Purple!" Frantically the Queen Mum waved her arms and tried to quiet them. Finally the blast of a trumpet split the air, and there was silence.

Color Wars banners decorated the Hall of Music. The two huge candelabras were specially fitted for score keeping.

They each held a hundred candles, one all purple, the other all crimson. The scores could range from one to five, which was the highest. The Queen Mum, Princess Roseanna, and the Master of the Hawks were the judges. There was always great tension as the scorekeeper footman walked silently with his long torch to light more candles.

Alicia sat glumly between Gundersnap and Kristen on the Purples' side of the hall. All the other princesses sat excitedly with their birds in their show cages. She was the only camper on either team without one.

Princess Morwenna was first on the stage for the Crimsons. "My bird is a silver blue-tipped squinch. They are known for doing their best songs at funerals. It shall sing a hymn."

"Whoopie!" muttered Kristen.

"*Glockschnotten ferkyn!*" exclaimed Gundersnap, which roughly translated from Slobo to "about as much fun as a snotty nose on a freezing day."

Three candles were lit when Morwenna's bird completed its song. Most of the princesses had gayer songs. By the time it was Princess Gundersnap's turn, no one had yet received a one. Nor had any princess's bird received a five. The Crimsons were in the lead.

Gundersnap was quite a hit as she and her little bird

marched about the stage. Her bird sang a rousing tune called "The March of the Fifth Artillery." The scorekeeper footman went to the Purple team's candelabra. Everyone held their breath as the footman continued on after lighting the third candle and then the fourth! Would there be a fifth? No. But still, a huge cheer burst out. The two teams were tied now. What was needed to break the tie was another high-scoring bird from the Purples. But the Purples were out of birds, and still the weeb was nowhere in sight.

The Queen Mum came back onto the stage. "I think everyone has performed except for our Princess Alicia?"

The entire audience turned to look at Alicia. She shrank down in her chair. A titter spread through the Crimson team. Even the Snort was smirking. Gundersnap squeezed her hand gently and said, "It's not your fault!" But just then Alicia felt something brush her shoulder.

Gundersnap gasped. "Your veeb!"

Alicia slid her eyes sideways. The golden bird was perched right on her shoulder. "You're back!" she whispered.

And the weeb opened his beak. A beautiful song unfurled in the air like a ribbon of gold. Alicia straightened and then rose from her seat. The audience sat spellbound. Never had anyone heard such caroling. The bird itself seemed to sparkle. It was as if the sun shone from the Princess of All the Belgravias' shoulder. Her weeb sang and sang and sang.

When it finished, the judges conferred. The footman began his excruciatingly slow march toward the Purples' candelabra.

"One, two, three, four," members of the Purple team whispered to themselves. Did he stop? Did he slow? Would there be . . . ? Everyone sat at the edges of their chairs.

"Five!"

A tumultuous shriek rose from one side of the Hall of Music. Five new candle flames licked the darkness of the hall. The Purples had won the Color Wars!

The din of the Purple team princesses' screaming could be heard all the way to Camp Burning Shield.

Chapter 20

STITCHES IN A LONG NIGHT

Long after the concert had ended, while the castle slept, three princesses slipped through the shadows of the night to begin work on the tapestry. In the Portrait Gallery, they stopped in front of the painting of Princess Kyranala. Alicia touched the frame, and it swung open to reveal the door.

"This way," Alicia whispered to Gundersnap and Kristen. The three princesses began to climb the winding staircase. When they reached the top, Alicia showed them the tapestry. She held her candle up to the cloth, and with her finger traced the stitches she had completed. "You see, this is the ghost princess." She touched the figure in the tapestry. "And do you see the outline of this bird?"

Kristen and Gundersnap stepped closer. "It looks as if it is half in and half out of the cage," Gundersnap said.

"Yes, I know. You see, we must stitch it to find the answer."

"Look at that princess's headgear!" Kristen whispered. "And the veil. It's so Middle Ages!"

They felt a cool breeze stir the air. She's coming, Alicia thought.

"But of course, dear, it was the Middle Ages," a voice said. The three princesses whirled around to see Princess Kyranala.

"I brought my turretmates, Your Highness, as you suggested. We are ready to sew."

"Yes, Your Highness, vee are here to report for duty." Gundersnap gave a little salute.

"Is the bird in the cage or out of the cage?" Kristen asked. "We can't tell."

"He is in more than just a cage," Princess Kyranala replied mysteriously.

What did she mean, more than just a cage? Alicia wondered.

"Free him, my dears, free him!" she urged.

"Free him from what? Will he fly away forever?" Alicia asked.

"No. He will fly to me," Princess Kyranala replied softly.

"He is your veeb?" Gundersnap asked.

"He is my knight."

"Your knight? Sir Roland?" Alicia gasped. "The one you wrote to in *Love Letters of a Forgotten Princess*? The bird is Sir Roland?

"Yes," Princess Kyranala said. "Remember, I told you that Guthstab had ordered his death. Berwynna turned him into a bird so he could fly away and escape. She brought him to the Forest of Chimes."

"But why didn't she turn him back into a knight?" Alicia asked.

"Berwynna's magic is great, but it is not perfect. He was trapped. Nothing Berwynna did could break the spell. We tried everything to bring him back. But when you arrived that first night, when you opened your favorite book and began to read about the Forgotten Princess and we found that you understood the deep love I had for my knight, the transformation slowly began."

"But couldn't you go to the forest and find him and release him yourself?" Alicia asked.

"I had tried. And I had tried to stitch the rest of the tapestry, but the ghosts of restless spirits need more. We needed you, a living princess, one who believed in us. When we saw you loved our book, we knew you were the one.

"And now you can help him complete the journey." She smiled and held up three needles, one with golden thread and two with turquoise. She handed the two with turquoise threads to Gundersnap and Kristen and the one with golden thread to Alicia.

"What are we supposed to do?" Kristen asked.

But Alicia knew exactly. "'The song is not the end in sight; For this you need to stitch a knight,'" she recited.

"But you must begin by stitching the bird," Princess Kyranala said.

"Yes, the bird. We must free the weeb so it might become a knight," Alicia said.

The three princesses stitched until the moon climbed high in the sky and the soft spring air turned to summer and then to autumn. The rustle of crisp leaves could be heard outside the turret window.

At last Alicia poked her needle in for the very last stitch of the bird. A shimmer seemed to glow from within the tapestry. The bird they had just finished began to lengthen into a human form, and its cage became shining armor. At that moment the shutters flew open, and on the autumn breeze red and golden leaves tumbled into the turret room. They swirled about as if caught in a gale and then, just as Princess Kyranala had stepped from the ashes and flames of the fire, a knight stepped from the leaves. He wore golden armor, and on his shoulders were turquoise flowers.

He knelt in front of the ghost princess. "I am here, dear one."

The princess opened her mouth to speak, but she could not. Tears began to stream down her face, leaving silver paths on her cheeks.

The knight then turned to the three princesses. "I am forever in your debt, Princesses," he said. "And my dear Princess Gundersnap?"

"*Ja?*" Gundersnap looked slightly alarmed.

"I even forgive you for shaking me like a saltshaker."

Gundersnap put her hands to her face, which was turning quite red. They all began to giggle.

"No harm done, my dear. No harm done," Sir Roland said in a deep, kind voice.

For as thrilled as Alicia was when her songbird had finally sung that evening, this indeed was even more thrilling. It wasn't the fact that the bird had finally sung and the Purples had won the Color Wars. Those desires of hers all seemed so small and so selfish by comparison to what had just happened—a knight and his lady had been reunited. Now they were two spirits put to rest, inseparable.

"For eternity," Sir Roland said as he embraced his princess.

"For eternity," Princess Kyranala replied.

And then, as quickly as each had appeared, they now dissolved into the mist of the early morning.

That was the last the three princesses of the South Turret saw of the Princess Kyranala and her knight, Sir Roland. The princesses went back the following evening to look at the tapestry, hoping that perhaps there might be some hint about where the lovers had gone. But there was none. Alicia touched the stitching lightly. "I guess the tapestry is finished. The story told." She sighed.

But Princess Gundersnap was looking at another part of the tapestry. She squinted hard. What was she seeing? Was it a horse? No, not exactly. A unicorn? But unicorns weren't real. Unicorns were just made-up creatures from fairy tales. Fairy tales weren't practical.

As a practical girl and daughter of one of the most powerful rulers on earth, Gundersnap had had it drummed into her since birth that certain things were silly, such as reading fairy tales. Unicorns would definitely come under that heading. Unicorns weren't practical in the least. No, a princess needed a fine pony, or a great warhorse like Thunder Monster, her mother's charger. Gundersnap squinted harder. This tapestry was far from finished, she suddenly realized. But unicorns? Impossible.

Still . . .